D0502702

PLAYING A DANGEROUS GAME

PLAYING A DANGEROUS GAME

PATRICK OCHIENG

ACCORD BOOKS

NORTON YOUNG READERS

An Imprint of W. W. Norton & Company
Independent Publishers Since 1923

For Carol, Ian, and Jairus: the three pillars of my life.
And for Mum and Dad.

For information about permission to reproduce selections from this book, write to
Permissions, W. W. Norton & Company, Inc., 500 Fifth Avenue, New York, NY 10110

For information about special discounts for bulk purchases, please contact
W. W. Norton Special Sales at specialsales@wwnorton.com or 800-233-4830

Manufacturing by LSC Communications, Harrisonburg
Production manager: Beth Steidle

Library of Congress Cataloging-in-Publication Data
Names: Ochieng, Patrick, author.
Title: Playing a dangerous game / Patrick Ochieng.
Description: First edition. | New York : Accord Books/Norton Young Readers, [2021] |
Audience: Ages 9–12. | Summary: In 1970s Kenya, ten-year-old Lumush and his three
friends discover a criminal operation that puts both themselves and their families in danger.
Identifiers: LCCN 2021023089 | ISBN 9781324019138 (hardcover) |
ISBN 9781324019145 (epub)
Subjects: CYAC: Friendship—Fiction. | Smuggling—Fiction. | Adventure and adventurers—
Fiction. | Blacks—Kenya—Fiction. | Kenya—History—20th century—Fiction. |
LCGFT: Action and adventure fiction.
Classification: LCC PZ7.1.O1985 Pl 2021 | DDC [Fic]—dc23
LC record available at https://lccn.loc.gov/2021023089

W. W. Norton & Company, Inc., 500 Fifth Avenue, New York, N.Y. 10110
www.wwnorton.com

W. W. Norton & Company Ltd., 15 Carlisle Street, London W1D 3BS

2 4 6 8 9 0 7 5 3 1

CHAPTER ONE

✳ ✳ ✳

MAMA IS ALL SMILES. She rubs her hands together and runs her tongue against her lips. She does that when she is excited.

"The opportunity to join Hill School doesn't come every day," she shouts louder than the railway siren, and you would think she'd won the lottery.

Baba has been promoted. The day before yesterday he came back from work waving a yellow letter that said he was now a manager.

"Oh Lord, shelter your servant from all those who would wish him harm," Mama went down on her knees and prayed when she saw Baba's promotion letter, and we had no option but to follow suit. "Shelter him under your wing, oh Lord. Scatter all the doubting Thomases to the four corners of the earth. And Lord now that your servant has been promoted it is only right that he gets one of those management houses, up on the hill . . ." She went on and on, stopping only after Baba loudly cleared his throat.

The very next day, a Friday, my younger sister, Awino, and I sit the Hill School admission interview and pass. Me, I suspect

1

those snobs of Hill School just wanted to see who they are admitting into their posh school.

They allow us a whole week to make preparations before starting at Hill School, but Mama insists that we get all the stuff we need early enough.

"Saturday would be a good day to do the shopping," she says.

"Why not wait until Monday when all the shops are open," Baba suggests, and Mama reluctantly agrees.

She spends the weekend writing a list of what she says will make us look like real Hill School kids.

IT'S MONDAY MORNING, and though shops in town do not open their doors until eight, Mama wakes us up at dawn. I rub the sleep from my eyes and watch Deno curled up in a ball under his blanket and envy him. Deno is twelve, two years older than me. He is in Standard 7 and will be doing his final exams this year, so Baba thought it wouldn't be a good idea for him to change schools. He'll be staying on at St. Josephs Primary School.

I head for the bathroom, but Awino is already at the door, a towel wrapped around her head.

"Please let your little sister go first," Mama says after Awino's shouting attracts her attention. You would think Mama is requesting, but me, I know it's an order that can be enforced with a smack, so I let Awino use the bathroom first, and she stays in there forever.

Mama's threats finally get her out.

Eight on the dot and we are off with Mama striding ahead. She stops at the foot of the rail overpass, to take Awino's hand. She grabs out for mine but I'm too quick for her. But she gets a grip on my hand when we approach a white, gated house on Desai Street that has remained unoccupied for years, ever since a white woman and her daughter died mysteriously in it. Mama drags us to the opposite side of the street, like the house is a threat.

"The further one stays from that evil house, the better," she whispers, and increases her pace.

I steal a glimpse of the imposing house behind an unkempt hedge. A tall zambarau tree sways above its rusty iron roof.

"Mama?"

"Yes, Awino?"

"Is it true a girl and her mother died in that house? And that the girl's father later committed suicide?" she glances over her shoulder.

"You are too small to be talking about such things," Mama drags her forward.

"Are there ghosts in that house?" Awino persists.

"Now who has been feeding you that nonsense?"

"Deno says . . ."

"Wait until we get back home, then I'll teach that stupid brother of yours to stop filling your mind with such stories," Mama says, and I'm glad I'm not the one who told Awino about the ghost house.

MOST OF THE SHOPS are opening when we get to River Road, which Baba often says is the heart of Nairobi city. Cars are already speeding up and down, their horns blaring.

"You keep pulling your hand away and those crazy bus drivers will run you over," Mama makes another grab for my hand.

I'd rather some bus ran me over than be seen by my friends as I'm dragged all over the place by my mother, I tell myself. Of course, I don't say it out loud. If I did, I'd be dead, and it would not be because some crazy bus driver ran over me. Mama would beat them to it.

People are selling all sorts of stuff. They walk about, waving their wares in your face: combs, pens, books, cups, glasses—everything you can think of. Others are on the sidewalk, polishing shoes or shaving hair. They shout out offers for all manner of services. They argue, shout, and even scream out. They use different tones to sell their wares and it sounds like one big band with musicians playing different instruments and singing different songs at the same time.

Mama says the pickpockets of River Road can make away with your socks without removing your shoes, as if that were even possible. She stops to wag her forefinger at a thin man in an oversize brown jacket, who smiles, winks, and slinks away.

"The fool thinks he can steal from me? I've lived in this town for so long I can spot a 'pickie' from a mile." Mama clucks and makes us increase our pace.

A small crowd has gathered around a man rolling a die on a board. He covers the die with a plastic cup and deftly moves two other cups on a board. "Hapa pata, hapa potea," he shouts and invites onlookers to place bets over which cup hides the die. Me, I think I have it figured out but Mama drags us across the road.

"Only crooks and fools play pata potea," she says, like she has read my mind. "You can never win."

After lots of shoving and sidestepping we stop outside a shop with pictures of some white boys and girls in school uniforms and the words PERFECT UNIFORM FITTERS on a sign above its doorway.

Why can't they have pictures of Black kids? Maybe the painter doesn't know how to paint them. The pictures we draw in school are also of kids with straight hair and pinched noses. It's easier to draw such pictures because the books we read have such pictures.

The shop owner chats Mama like they have known each other all their lives. He says he once lived in Nyanza and had a shop in a dusty village called Kwa Wahindi. He wishes he had stayed there, where people were honest and not "crooks" like they are in the city.

Mama points out the items she wants, and the shop owner shouts orders to a wiry man who clambers up a rickety ladder and uses a forked stick to bring them down from the shelves.

"This one isn't gray enough. That's not the white I want. Which mosquito were these socks made for? No one is that small. I said white, not cream," Mama goes on and on and I'm thinking if the shop owner does not reach over the counter to strangle her, the wiry man will most certainly smash his forked stick on her head.

Soon enough everything is piled on the counter and you would think we are about to buy every item in the shop.

Mama sifts through the mountain of clothes, chooses what she wants, and the wiry man struggles up his ladder to return the rest. Then the price battle begins.

"That will be twenty-five shillings," the man says when Mama inquires about the price of a gray skirt for Awino.

"You must think I'm mad to pay that for cloth with a few stitches running through it," Mama narrows her eyes.

"The factory in Jinja is closed, mama. Amin sent everyone away. This is coming straight from India."

"I'm still not paying twenty-five shillings for it."

"How much you are willing to give?" he asks, but Mama is already on another item.

"How much do you want for those faded gray shorts?"

"Those are best quality. I sell at twenty-two shillings, but for you, my very good customer, I will give at twenty only. It's best price."

"Eish! Someone thinks I print money."

"How much you will pay for the trouser?" the man asks.

"Five shillings," Mama says without as much as a twitch on her face.

"You want me to close my shop? You want me to go back to Kwa Wahindi to sell kerosene? I will give you for fifteen shillings, throwaway price. That is what I purchased it at."

"I'll pay nine for the skirt and ten for the shorts," Mama says.

"Okay, I will take fifteen shillings for the trouser and ten for the skirt. How many piece you are buying?" he says, but Mama is already dragging us out.

"Come back, mama! Fine, I will give at your price, but you must not tell anyone."

Mama reaches under her blouse for her purse and unzips it to reveal a smaller one. She pays the shop owner, who looks relieved to see the last of her. He pinches Awino's cheeks, hands her sweets, and pretends to smile.

He smells of cigarettes and onions.

WE STOP OUTSIDE a Bata shoe shop that says: FIXED PRICES NO BARGAINING. Still, Mama asks the frowning shop attendant for a discount. They make me try on different shoes before settling on two pairs, both a size too big.

"Your feet will grow into them," Mama says, as if I'm supposed to wear the pair for a decade.

Hungry and tired we struggle home, where Mama makes us dress up and parade about like models, with Apondi passing comments. Apondi is from Mama's shaggs and has lived with us for as long as I can remember. Mama says she is her sister, but then everyone who comes from Mama's village in Alego is her sister or brother.

For the millionth time, Mama reminds us that Hill School is not St. Josephs, where they allow you to dress in rags. "Remember, everyone is watching." She looks me up and down as I struggle out of my new undershirt and shoes. "Your father is now a manager and you have to look the part. And you, Lumush, I don't want to see you running around the estate in torn sneakers, with your wild friends," Mama warns.

I wonder how that will even be possible. Other than Awino

and me, the only other kid in Hill School who's from Railway Estate is Roba. So where does Mama expect me to find new friends to play with in the estate?

Those thoughts just stay in my head. No reason to allow them to grow into words.

CHAPTER TWO

✱ ✱ ✱

IT'S WEDNESDAY EVENING, a couple of days before I report to
Hill School. I'm with my friends hanging out at our favorite spot
behind the estate, near an old Zephyr car that rests on stones.
They have just come from school and are still in uniform.

"You think those snobs will welcome you in that posh school
of theirs?" Odush sniggers. "They'll probably wash their hands
with soap every time you greet them," he slaps palms with Mose
then tries to do the same with Dado.

Dado ignores him.

Odush, Dado, and Mose are my best friends. We are neighbors
at Railway Estate. Odush is a class ahead of the rest of us at St.
Josephs, but he still hangs out with us.

"Remember the time the snobs from Hill School came to St.
Josephs for a debate? They brought their own food, stuck out their
noses in the air, like our school was stinking," Mose pinches his
nose and sniffs loudly. "They even refused to drink the soda we
offered them. We ended up drinking it all after they left."

"And they were not as smart as they made themselves out to be. We licked them in the debate," Dado says.

"I'm not interested in joining that stupid school," I laugh, as if I have a choice. But then what am I supposed to say?

"And you think you have a choice? Once your parents decide, that's it," Dado says, as though he has read my mind.

"I hear there are students who drive cars at that school." Mose widens his eyes.

"And how would I know? I'm not even in Hill School yet," I say, but I've also heard about students revving up in slick cars at Hill School, though I still don't believe it.

"You could arrive there pushing a hand cart," Odush laughs. "At least you'd have a set of wheels."

"You think that's funny, you loud mouth?"

Odush talks too much. Though he is taller and stronger than the rest of us, whenever there's trouble it's his heels we see. He can take off faster than those Americans do in the one-hundred-meter sprints. In a tight spot, I'd rather have Dado by my side, anytime. Mose, on the other hand, loves to clown around. He never takes anything seriously.

"Hey! I hear they even have a swimming pool in that crazy school," Mose says and rolls his eyes.

"Better not try out the river style you learned in shaggs. Those show-offs would laugh you right out of the pool," Odush says, and even Dado laughs.

"I've been to the Railway Club pool. I know how to swim," I protest.

"Some of those kids at Hill School probably have pools in their homes," Dado says.

"And when are you people moving up the hill now that your father is a boss?" Odush sticks out his stomach.

"Who said we were moving?"

"But all bosses stay up the hill. You can't stay here now," Odush spreads his arms.

"You want to see something good?" Dado changes the subject, to my relief. He removes a glossy magazine poster from under his shirt and spreads it out on the Zephyr's hood. It has half a dozen girls in colorful bikinis, standing by a pool.

"Wa, wa, wa," Mose goes, and Odush tries to snatch it, but he's not fast enough.

Me, I'm just glad we're not talking about Hill School anymore.

CHAPTER THREE

✻ ✻ ✻

IT'S FRIDAY MORNING, the day we are to report to our new school. I don't even know why we have to go on Friday. Couldn't it wait until Monday? But try telling that to my mama. She escorts us all the way to the huge metal gate at the school's entrance.

"Now remember, everyone will be watching, so you better be on your best behavior. Don't you start acting wild like that boy who lives in a kiosk with his father . . . what's his name again? The one who doesn't go to school? Oh yes, Zgwembe," Mama warns.

"Yes, Ma."

"And you must speak in English at all times."

I nod.

"Make sure you take care of your little sister."

I nod again.

I glance over my shoulder to watch her receding form. I then resign myself to my fate and allow myself to be swallowed behind the huge pine hedge that surrounds Hill School. You'd think someone just sat down with watercolors and painted Hill School on a canvas, complete with neat sidewalks, trees, and buildings. The school's imposing administration building stares out at you like you are an intruder. You never get a chance to stare back, though, because a frowning prefect stands there to find fault with everything you are wearing. Either your tie isn't properly knotted or your socks aren't pulled up high enough.

Awino is almost in tears because a prefect says the top button of her blouse is not done. She tries to fit the button in but the buttonhole is too small.

I step over to help, but another prefect points his forefinger at me and waves me along.

AT HILL SCHOOL the first activity before classes begin is the morning parade in the quadrangle. Once we are gathered there, two unsmiling prefects march past like they are inspecting a guard of honor. After a short prayer, we sing the national anthem:

"*Oh God of all creation.*

Bless this, our land and Nation . . ." we chorus out.

Though I've never memorized all the words, I move my lips in sync with the others. I am convinced that no one can tell I'm faking until my eyes fall upon a tall prefect staring straight at me, like he can read my mind.

Our class teacher is a portly white man called Bumbles. He wears a brown tweed coat and walks like he is floating above the ground. He speaks through his nose, swallowing most of his words. He does not waste any time in showing that he dislikes me.

"You can fool the others, but not me. I will be watching your every step. Import any of your filthy habits to Hill School and you'll have me to reckon with," he warns.

He calls me something that sounds like "Loper." Soon enough I find out the word is "interloper." That's someone who doesn't belong, like a gate-crasher. I guess the "inter" gets lost somewhere in between Bumbles's thin lips and his golden mustache. I kind of like the sound of the word, though I don't like what it means.

It's in the attitude of the other pupils, this interloper thing. It's in their looks and their smiles too. They clear their throats each time I approach and the accusation is all over their faces. They exchange knowing glances before they talk to me. I'd love to say I don't care but I do.

Even Roba, who only joined Hill School a couple of months ago, treats me like an interloper. He too has an accusing look on his face, though he must have been treated the same way when he first joined Hill School.

IT'S MY THIRD DAY IN HILL SCHOOL, a Tuesday, yet it already feels like a whole year. I'm exhausted from trying to figure out all that's going on around me. I'm walking toward the school lab, when a voice booms out from behind:

"Some of us have no intention of getting anywhere before the sun goes down."

I turn around and it's the headmaster with his eyes fixed on me.

"If I were you, I would put some urgency into that walk," the Headie says, and I'm off, like the ghosts in the deserted house on Desai Street are after me.

The Headie teaches English language and says "English is King"—and God help you if he catches you speaking in "those native languages." He goes on and on about discipline and makes it sound like it is three separate words: "disc-i-pline." After a long lecture on "disc-i-pline" he moves on to "clean-li-ness," which he says is next to "God-li-ness." I wonder why he teaches English, when there are actual Englishmen like Bumbles in Hill School. They might as well have Bumbles teaching Kiswahili.

A LANKY BOY named Kazungu sits in front of me in class. I can't figure out how he keeps his shirt sparkling white the whole week. He keeps peering over his shoulder like he is scared I might harm him.

Kazungu's father is an assistant minister. It's the reason Bumbles goes all soft when talking to him. He is dropped off at school each morning in a shiny black car. His uniform looks like he just picked it off the shelf at the PERFECT UNIFORM FITTERS. Maybe he has a new set for every day of the month.

Kazungu always has money, which he uses to treat his friends at the school shop. Other than a girl called Lillian, who sits next to him and makes no secret of her dislike for him, the other students in Standard 5A act like lapdogs around him. They laugh at what he says even when it isn't funny.

Me, I think Kazungu is daft and covers it up with his money.

WE ARE IN HISTORY CLASS, the last class of the day. Bumbles has been droning on and on about an explorer called David Livingstone and his faithful porters. No one is listening to Bumbles anymore, because it's Friday and our minds are already tuned to the coming weekend. But the final bell just won't ring.

Kazungu lifts his hand to catch the teacher's attention, and I'm thinking the show-off probably wants everybody to know how good he is in history.

"Yes, Kazungu," Bumbles says.

"Some money is missing from my bag."

"What? How much?" Bumbles puts on a solemn face.

"Twenty shillings," Kazungu says.

I'm wondering how anyone could have a whole twenty shillings in school.

"You are certain the money was in your bag?" Bumbles asks. His eyes are already peering in my direction.

Kazungu nods.

"Does anyone know anything about Kazungu's money?"

"*No!*" we all chorus, and still Bumbles's eyes do not leave me.

"Maybe he should learn to take better care of his money," Lillian says in her soft, measured tone, taking Bumbles and everyone else by surprise. Lillian is the brightest student in our class.

"For the last time, does anyone know anything about the lost money?" Still Bumbles eyes me.

"Why would anyone come to school with so much money? How would we even know if he had it in the first place?" Lillian again interjects.

"If you go on like that, I'll mark you down for detention, Lillian," Bumbles warns. Just then, the last bell goes.

I would never take anyone's money because that's stealing. I wouldn't even know what to do with twenty shillings if I had it. But who is going to believe me? Who else but the interloper would do such a terrible thing? I'm thinking out all these thoughts when my eyes fall on Lillian. She is smiling at me, and the look on her face tells me she knows I'd never do such a thing. It means the world to me.

CHAPTER FOUR

✱ ✱ ✱

I REALLY LOOK FORWARD TO the weekends. Now that I have changed schools, Saturdays and Sundays are even more valuable. It's the only time I get to hang out with Dado and the gang. Of course, we can still meet in the evening after school, like today, but that's only for a short time before Mama sends for me.

Odush's eyes trail me as I approach the old Zephyr car. Dado is sitting on the hood with Mose next to him. I've been contemplating telling them about Kazungu's lost money and how Bumbles acts like I stole it. But maybe it's not such a good idea. Dado would most probably sympathize, but I know Odush would make fun of me.

"That's another pair of shoes you are wearing," Odush stares at my shoes.

"This is the same old pair I've always worn. I polished them in the morning," I lie and kick out at the dust, to show it is no big deal. All the while, I'm praying my shoes don't get scratched. Mama would kill me if they did.

"Who can't see those shoes are fresh from Bata? And I can see you are also wearing an undershirt," Odush sneers.

"And what's wrong with wearing an undershirt?"

"What is it with you people? It's like you have never seen new shoes or an undershirt before," Dado interjects.

"He's showing off when just the other day he had only one pair of old, torn school shoes. But now his father is a . . ." Odush continues, but I'm having no more of it.

I go for him and it is only because Dado steps in between us that I don't punch him.

I'm never wearing any of this new stuff again. I don't care if I don't look the part, as Mama would have it. After all, I didn't ask Baba to go and become a manager, and no one asked me if I wanted to change schools.

I miss St. Josephs and its roughly cast walls, its dusty compound. I miss the ball games, the roasted groundnuts sold by the woman in a blue flowing dress and a big silver cross dangling from her neck. I miss the games at break, with no stern-faced prefects calling for calm and order. The sim-sim balls, the roasted maize, the not-too-ripe mangoes sprinkled with ground pepper, sold through the gaps in the school fence. But now I am in Hill School and not St. Josephs, where Cleophus the bell ringer used a metal rod to hammer away at an old metal rim dangling from a tree to signal the end of break, and students with soiled collars, dusty shoes, and socks that never stayed up dashed about like wildebeests in the Mara.

Hill School—as our Headie always reminds us—is about order and disc-i-pline, and anyone who can't handle that can leave.

But that's easier said than done. It is difficult when you have
to cross over from Railway Estate to Hill School. It's like two
different countries, where people speak different languages and
you have to switch tongues each time you cross over from one
to the other. One moment you are standing in an orderly queue
at Hill School, speaking in hushed tones and saying "washroom"
instead of "toilet" and "please" and "thank you" to people you
should be telling to go jump under a train. The next moment you
are with friends, tearing across the estate using words that would
make Bumbles's face turn pink, screaming at the top of your voice
and generally having a great time.

Sometimes I slip and say things the way I shouldn't, and when
it happens at Hill School everyone looks at me like I crawled out
of a sewer.

It's confusing.

It's hard.

What makes it harder, though, is when I'm in the estate with
my friends and they think I'm showing off.

"Lumush?" I hear Apondi shout even before she appears at the
far end of Block 1. "Your mum wants you this very moment."

"Coming," I shout back. If it wasn't that I needed to get away
from Odush, I wouldn't respond so fast. I hurry after Apondi to
find Mama waiting at our front door.

"I need two packets of milk from Mama Nandwa's kiosk," she

hands me a five-shilling note. She doesn't say anything else but her look spurs me off like a starter gun.

I already have Mama's milk when I spot Njish approaching Mama Nandwa's kiosk.

"Sasa," I greet her but she does not respond. I know she's come from church because she is all dressed up. I think about telling her that Mama urgently needs the milk I'm carrying, but realize it's not a good idea. It's the first time I've seen her since I moved from St. Josephs.

Njish used to sit in front of me in class at St. Josephs. My eyes would never leave her cornrowed hair. It was like she knew, because she would abruptly turn around to find me staring. But then how was I to avoid looking at someone I liked a lot? Someone who was right in front of me? Each time our eyes met, I would feel like I'd been caught cheating on an exam. But that didn't stop me. Her, she would just roll her big round eyes and smile.

Njish was fond of passing me notes with neat, painted hearts. I would grab them from under the desk and shove them into my pocket, too scared to read them in class. I would read them afterwards. Once, I dropped one of the notes before I could pocket it and our teacher, Wamalwa, picked it up.

"Now, who wrote this note?" "Teacher Focus"—for that was Wamalwa's nickname—raised it for all to see.

The whole class was silent.

"I'll ask again. Who wrote this note?"

Still silence.

"Lumumba? I know you have something to do with this note because I found it next to your desk. But because I'm not sure, I will punish the whole class. And as for you, Wanjiru, you better concentrate on your studies instead of passing notes to boys."

Njish's full name is Wanjiru, but she loves being called Njish.

Now Njish's eyes are directed heavenward and her hands are planted firmly on her hips. "You have been avoiding me since you moved to that hopeless school," she tilts her head to the side.

"No!" I shake my head.

"Tell me, do you have a girlfriend in that school? The truth, Lumush, tell me the truth."

I shake my head and try to maintain a serious look, but I can feel the edges of my mouth curve out into a smile.

"You are lying. I know you are."

I force the smile away and fish out my most serious look, and that seems to satisfy Njish.

"Promise you will not have another girlfriend except me?"

"I promise."

"Cross your heart."

"Cross my heart."

"Even when those useless girls of Hill School throw themselves at you, promise you will tell them you are not interested," Njish says, and I almost burst out laughing because I'm as scared as hell of those Hill School girls who are always rolling their eyes and sniffing the air like everything stinks. Except for Lillian, who I think is nice. But I'd be crazy to tell Njish about how Lillian stood up for me.

"Promise, Lumush, promise?"

"I promise."

Assured I'm safe from those evil girls in Hill School, Njish hurries off to wherever it is she is headed for.

CHAPTER FIVE

* * *

MONDAY MORNING, and Bumbles is still eyeing me like I murdered someone.

Tuesday, and still the suspicious look.

On Wednesday, Kazungu announces he has found his money in one of the pockets of his backpack.

"It's only fair he apologizes to everyone," Lillian furrows her brow and stares in Kazungu's direction.

"That won't be necessary," Bumbles says. "No one was accused of taking Kazungu's money."

Oh! Really? With the looks I've had to endure, nobody accused anyone?

I stare in Bumbles's direction and he looks away.

"Has nobody ever told you it is rude to stare?" he says when he looks up and finds me still watching him.

Now see who is talking, I want to tell him, but I still do not speak. I just keep the thought safe in my head, far away from people like Bumbles. I'm getting good at keeping things in my head. I think them out, without voicing them. I have silent conversations no one else can hear. Later in the day I can talk to Dado and the others about most of the things, and we can have a good laugh.

That's how I keep out of trouble at Hill School.

A SQUINT-EYED PREFECT with Jumbo ears just won't let me be. Neat gold ribbons cut across the sleeve of his jacket. They are symbols of his authority. He has the power to stop, search, and confiscate. He always stops me, not because there is anything wrong but because he can. When he is in a foul mood—which is almost all the time—he looks me up and down and finds one fault or the other. If it isn't my tie, then it's my socks that are not right, or my shoes are not polished. I'm sure that, even if I were to walk straight out of the uniform shop in River Road with brand-new everything, the guy would still find something wrong.

Soon enough, I discover his weakness. The next time he stops me I stare straight into his squinting eyes, and he quickly looks away.

I guess I'm dismissed.

JUMBO EARS CORNERS ME near the school shop and snatches my warm mandazi. He already has about half a dozen mandazis in a khaki packet, most probably confiscated from the other students.

The next time he stops me, I spit all over my mandazi and make to hand it to him.

He clucks and waves me away.

Jumbo Ears is not the only weirdo in Hill School. There is this boy called Maanzo who has huge Popeye arms that threaten to burst right out of his sleeves and acts like he stepped right out of a comic book. He walks with jerky steps like any moment his limbs will come loose at the joints.

"And who are you?" he asks when he first corners me next to the locker rooms.

"Nonsense!" he shouts, when I whisper out my name. "You are not Lumumba. You are a 'mono.' And do you know what a mono is?"

I shake my head, and Popeye arms is only too willing to educate me.

"A mono is a gibbon, with a long curved tail which is invisible to all monos but visible to seniors like me. And it is up to me as a senior to see to it that this creature is brought back to human culture through medulla-striking."

I'm still struggling to understand what it's all about, when I receive a sharp rap to the head, probably to bring me back to human culture. From then on I look out for this lunatic and stay out of his way.

WITH ALL ITS WEIRDOS, bullies, and show-offs, there are still some great guys in Hill School, like Rashid.

Rashid is the biggest boy in our school. He makes Jumbo Ears—who is much taller than the rest of us—look like a toddler. The difference, though, is that, unlike JE, Rashid never gets in anyone's way. For a guy his size, his handshake is gentle and he always has a smile on his face. You feel comfortable around this giant, who barely speaks.

Rush, as everyone knows him, minds his own business. Despite his awesome size, he never tries to push anyone around. He has a beard that we all find hilarious because it comprises only a few hairs that dot his chocolate-brown chin. He loves to pinch it and smile.

He prefers the back row during morning parade, but is still visible from the front. I've never once seen a prefect or teacher raise their voice at Rush or punish him. Perhaps the need never arises. But me, I think they are all intimidated by the guy's size. At least the prefects are.

One morning during break, as I'm heading for the locker rooms, I see Rush go down like someone has chopped off his legs from under him. He tumbles awkwardly to the ground and begins to kick and tremble as though something urgently needs to exit his body.

A crowd of students soon gathers around Rush.

"Everyone move back," Jumbo Ears asserts his authority and bulldozes through. He kneels down and presses Rush to the ground, trying to restrain his kicking and trembling.

"Don't do that," I push him aside, surprising even myself. "You don't do that when someone is having a seizure unless there is something around them that might hurt them," I echo what I once heard Baba say.

I wait a moment for Rush to calm before I roll him to his side to clear his airways. After he regains his senses, I help him up and lead him through the staring crowd of students.

Rush flashes out a weak smile as I help him to his desk. There and then I can tell we will be friends.

And who doesn't need a friend like Rush in a place like Hill School?

AFTER YESTERDAY'S INCIDENT, I can't wait to get back to school. I haven't forgotten the admiring looks I received from my classmates as I took care of Rush.

I arrive at school early and gingerly walk up to Jumbo Ears who is standing at the gate. Though I know he has had it in for me since I joined Hill School, I have a feeling yesterday's events made things worse, when I showed him up by taking charge during Rush's seizure.

Jumbo Ears shoves his hand into my backpack and almost immediately pulls it back out. His inspection seems quicker than usual. He gestures me away, and though I'm surprised I sling my bag onto my back and start to walk away.

"I want you in the PR this very moment," Jumbo Ears suddenly swivels, snaps his fingers, and points at me.

Wait a minute. The guy just inspected my bag and dismissed me. What is it now? I'm still wading through these thoughts when he follows up in a grating tone:

"You heard what I said, Lumumba, I want you in the prefects' room"; this time he is more specific and it surprises me he even knows my name. I walk up the gravel drive and cut across the quadrangle, all the while trying to figure out what awaits me.

Tucked between the school shop and the locker rooms, the PR, as everyone knows it, is out of bounds except through invitation by a prefect. I've heard lots of scary stories about the place.

I'm about to turn the brass knob of the door to the PR when I'm pushed right into the dimly lit room. I stumble forward, almost losing my balance.

"Now give me that bag," Jumbo Ears, who must have been following closely, yanks at my backpack and sends me sprawling on the floor.

"But you already checked my bag," I protest.

"You stay down and shut up," he shouts and empties the contents of my bag onto the floor. He bends down and makes a show of searching through the pile of books. "Aha! I knew it was you all along." He straightens up, brandishing a magnifying glass. "And you thought you would never be caught," he waves it in my face.

"That thing wasn't in my bag."

"Now you are accusing me of lying?"

"No. But I have no idea how that thing got there," I shout, and I can feel tears welling up in my eyes.

"You heard the Headie announce at the parade that the biology lab was losing equipment every day. Wait until he hears that you are the one stealing from the lab." Jumbo Ears waves the magnifying glass in my face, and then he is suddenly staring past me.

"That's enough," I hear someone say in a steady voice, and I turn around to find Rush standing behind me with his hands in his pockets. "I know you planted that thing in Lumumba's bag and I'm ready to swear before the Headie that I saw you do it," Rush says.

Jumbo Ears hangs his head and fixes his eyes on the floor. "Why are you interfering in what does not concern you?"

"Because Lumumba is my friend."

Rush turns to me and says, "Now gather your stuff and let's get out of this place."

I could hug him for that.

CHAPTER SIX

✳ ✳ ✳

MAMA NEVER STOPS reminding Baba to find a house on the hill. She has some of our things packed in cartons, but now that it is taking longer than expected she unpacks them. She never stops talking about having a house with a compound and her own vegetable patch.

"I don't know where this country is headed," Baba says. He is sitting in his favorite green chair next to the Grundig record player. He grabs a newspaper from the table, snaps it open, and buries his head behind it. "Those crooks at headquarters want a bribe before they give us a house up the hill? There is no way I'm going to give anyone even a cent. It's my right to be given one of those houses," he says from behind his newspaper.

"Why not give them what they want? Everyone is doing it," Mama says.

"That's corruption and I'll not be part of it," Baba's head momentarily peeps out from behind his paper.

"Remember the man who used to be in Block 5, the one

with the two huge dogs that used to bark endlessly? The one who worked with you at the yard and got promoted long after you?"

Baba's head peeps out a second time.

"He already has a house at the top of the hill. His wife sits with me in the Mothers' Union committee. She told me they gave a little something to the housing people."

"I thought that was un-Christian," he folds his paper on his lap. He has a sly twinkle in his eyes.

"It's what everyone is doing," Mama says again.

"They are no more than a bunch of hypocrites! But what do you expect? Lots of coffee would disappear while the man was on duty. His name was Mwenda, if I remember." Baba's paper goes up again and his head disappears behind it.

At times I wonder if he really reads his paper or if he just shelters behind it.

"WHAT DO YOU PEOPLE EAT in that posh school?" Odush asks one Friday after school.

"There's lots of stuff in the school shop," I say.

Odush raps his fingers against the Zephyr's rusted hood. He loves doing that and it's irritating. "I'm sure they don't have chili-sprinkled mangoes, like what Mama Maembe sells at St. Josephs."

"It's just a stupid kiosk," I try hard to show it's no big deal.

"Since he moved to that school he thinks he is better than all of us," Odush raises his nose up in the air.

"And who has stopped you from joining? They would probably

never let the likes of you past the gate," I say, losing my patience and taking him by surprise. That shuts him up.

I don't mind my friends poking fun at me about Hill School. Sometimes I join in, because my heart is still at St. Josephs. What I can't stand is Odush getting personal. It makes me feel like punching him.

CHAPTER SEVEN

✳ ✳ ✳

"TRUST AND OBEY

For there is no other way

To be happy . . ."

Apondi has been singing the same verse forever. Her singing is at times drowned out by the clanking sound of pots and pans banging against the kitchen sink. It's impossible to continue sleeping once Apondi begins washing and singing:

"Now that you are dead, will you be carrying your beautiful new bride to the grave with you?" she sings, and I'm wondering how one can carry anything after they are dead, let alone a bride.

It's Sunday morning and it feels great, because for a whole week I've slept in my own bed, which is unusual.

Most of the time Mama makes us give up our beds for relatives who just show up from shaggs lugging bags full of sweet potatoes and guavas, and babies tied to their backs. Some even come clutching live chickens under their arms as presents for Mama. Then Mama makes us give up our beds for the lumpy sofas in the living room.

Sometimes their snorty-nosed children wet our beds and the smell stays forever.

Some of them come for treatment in the big hospital named after the Father of the Nation. Mama makes Deno escort them there since they are too scared to cross the busy streets and he has to herd them like kids. Deno is always careful his friends do not see him.

Others come job hunting or kupiga lami, which means "to hit the tarmac," and they are the worst. They stay for weeks and head out every morning to the industrial area to look for work. At least that is what they say they do.

"How can someone come from so far to look for work?" I ask.

"They don't come to look for work, those crooks," Deno snorts.

"So where do they go to so early in the morning?"

"They go to Uhuru Park to sleep under trees until lunch time, when they hurry back to eat Mama's ugali."

"Why would someone come all the way from shaggs just to sleep under a tree in Uhuru Park?"

"You don't know those guys. They love the city and being able to brag about the tall buildings and the cars that zoom by when they go back home."

When they stay too long, Mama convinces them to leave, with a promise Baba will holler out if there is a job opening. Mama has already left for church, like she does every Sunday. Baba too leaves early. His job at the railway yard is an essential service and so he works on weekends.

Apondi never stops singing. She sings in the bathroom, in the kitchen, even when her mouth is full. If it is not a hymn, it's a nursery rhyme or one of those songs they play on VOK Radio:

"*Nyakonyakonyako*

Nyakonyakokonya . . ." Apondi repeats the words over and over again.

The song is by Congolese musicians, who dress in colorful bell-bottoms and put on so much makeup and perfume you can smell them from a mile away. They sing a blend of Lingala, Kiswahili, and sometimes even Luo.

Apondi knows the words of every song by heart. She knows all the songs they play on the VOK radio station. She even sings the songs that blare out from the bar next to the slaughterhouse, where tipsy men lean on a wooden counter and tear at huge chunks of roasted meat, which they wash down with beer from brown bottles with an elephant on the label. At night you can hear them sing out in slurred tones. It's like playing one of Baba's single vinyl records at 33 rpm. Mama says such men will never catch even a glimpse of God's heaven.

I remember a song about God's heaven . . .

I've got a shoe

You've got a shoe

All God's children got shoes

When I go to heaven gonna put on my shoe

Gonna walk all over God's heaven . . .

"APONDI, I'M STARVING. Can I have some tea?" I stand at the kitchen door and raise my voice above the din of her washing and singing.

"Apondi . . . Apondi . . . all the time. You think I'm a machine? Someone could think the sun will never rise, unless you call Apondi's name a hundred times."

She rolls her eyes and scowls.

Me, I'm not going anywhere. My stomach is rumbling like one of those Safari Rally cars found its way into it. Apondi can bite off my head for all I care, but I'm not leaving without breakfast.

"Apondi, could I . . ." I start again, but she doesn't let me get past those three words.

"I still have your dirty clothes to wash, yet here you are, pestering me about useless things like breakfast."

"But I'm hungry!"

"So what if you are hungry? Some people didn't even eat supper yesterday and they haven't died."

"Please!"

"Go fool someone else with those puppy-dog eyes. You are not getting anything from me and you can report me to your mother when she comes back. Then I can tell her what you and your stupid friends are up to."

I stretch out my arms to savor the heat from the charcoal jiko stove in the corner of the kitchen. It crackles and lets out tiny, glowing sparks that sting. I'm almost giving up when Apondi pours me a mug of tea and slaps two slices of bread on a saucer.

"And when you are through, you can go and play that silly game of pata potea with your silly friends, near that old car behind the block. It's where you idiots hatch all your naughty plans. As long as you hang around that old car, you will never make anything of your lives," she swears. "One of these days I'll talk to Mwachuma, ask him to cut that car into pieces and sell it as scrap metal in his yard," she threatens. Mwachuma is the old one-eyed man who operates a scrapyard at the edge of the estate and has a black dog called Tarzan.

Apondi speaks of the Zephyr like it's an evil thing that must be stopped before it ruins us.

CHAPTER EIGHT

✳ ✳ ✳

DADO AND MOSE ARE already seated on the Zephyr's hood, behind the estate. The grass around the rusted car has browned from being starved of sunlight.

Mose has his hands clenched into fists in front of him. "Pata, potea. Pata, potea," he sticks out one clenched fist after another and gestures me with his eyes, so I can pick the fist that has the ten-cent coin he has wagered, but I'm not interested.

Dado plays along and points out the wrong fist, losing his money with the bet.

"Pata, potea," Mose goes again, but Dado has had enough.

From the corner of my eye I see Odush approaching. He traveled to shaggs with his parents for the first-term school holidays. There is still a whole week before school resumes.

"When did you get back?" I ask, but Odush only clears his throat to catch the attention of the others.

He undoes the buttons on his shorts and pulls out his thing, and his face lights up in a smile. He holds it gingerly in his hand.

"It's cut!" Mose says, and we all draw close, eyes riveted.

Odush laughs all grown up–like. His laughter rolls inside his throat and bubbles out through his bared teeth. "It's how you become a man," he says.

"Who cut it for you?" Mose demands.

"Was it painful?" I ask.

"You! I know you would poop in your pants," he gestures in my direction and displays his big white teeth, like the Colgate toothpaste guy on the cover of Baba's magazine.

"Where is the piece they cut off?" Dado asks.

Odush ignores him.

"I saw my cousin Bura's thing after it was cut and it didn't look like yours."

Odush fixes Dado with an *"if you don't shut your big mouth, I'll shut it for you"* stare.

"Show us the piece they cut off," Dado persists.

"How would I know what the old guy did with all the pieces? There were twenty or so of us circumcised. And who says they give it to you after the cut?"

"Maybe he made samosas with it," Dado sniggers.

"One of these days I'll bash your silly head in," Odush says before slipping his thing back into his shorts.

"My mum promised to take me to a doctor to get mine cut," I lie.

"It's not the same thing. It must be done by the river with nothing for the pain. But now that your father is a manager you could have it done in the hospital with all the frilly stuff."

"Their people don't even cut—they just pull out teeth," Mose says.

"My mum says it's primitive to get cut with a rusty knife near a river like some people do. You could bleed to death, or get tetanus," Dado says.

"Tete . . . what?"

"It's what you get when you have a wound and you don't go for a jab," Dado says. His mother is a nurse at the railway dispensary so he knows such stuff.

"What does your Muuum know about getting cut?" Odush glowers. "Women don't get cut."

"Some women also get cut," Dado says, and we all look at him funny.

"What's there to cut?" We laugh.

"I don't know, but I've heard that some women get cut."

"I'll bet you screamed your head off when they did it," I say, and Odush swivels like he is about to punch me.

"I'm no crybaby like you. And why are you people still here in the estate when you should be in one of those huge houses, up the hill with those other snobs?" he says, and everyone laughs.

"And what are you laughing at?" I turn on Mose.

"But everyone laughed."

"It doesn't give you the right to laugh. And it wasn't me who decided to join that school. I don't even like being there."

"Let's go grab zambaraus from Desai Street," Dado suggests.

And we are off, past the abandoned mabati structure that once housed a barber shop. We zoom past the wall that stinks of pee, despite the sign that warns: NO URINATING ON THE WALL.

Once we get past the railway crossing sign, with the word DANGER emblazoned in red, we race up to the rail overpass.

Mose rushes up the steep stairs to the top of the overpass, then slides down its metal handrail and rushes up again. He does it over and over until we are on the other side. Then he sprints along Desai Street to catch up with us.

Cute houses peep out from behind Kei apple hedges along Desai Street. A short Asian man with a blue turban opens one of the ocher-painted gates, peers in our direction, then retreats. He reappears with a tall African man in well-pressed khaki pants. They gesture at us with bunched fists.

We don't stop to find out their intentions.

"Let's go get zambaraus from the tree in the compound of the abandoned house," Odush says.

"You mean the ghost house?" Mose says.

"I think that ghost stuff is just meant to scare people," Dado says.

"Are you saying the story of the white woman and her daughter dying in that house is fake? And what about the husband, who committed suicide after that? Is that also made up?" I ask.

"They could have died in there but that doesn't mean there are ghosts."

"What about the sounds people say they've heard coming from in there, and the lights they've seen going on and off at night? Apondi says she once heard the sound of something being dragged on the ground and that of a child crying—probably the ghost of the dead girl," I say.

"And what was Apondi doing on Desai Street at night?" Dado asks.

"She was escorting one of her friends who had visited."

"I don't see anything like ghosts in there," Dado points at the deserted house, "only juicy zambaraus. I can already feel them in my mouth. Who is coming along?"

I want to tell Dado and the others about Mama calling the house an evil place and how she seemed scared when we passed it, but I decide it's not a good idea. I don't want them thinking my mother is a coward.

It's zambarau season and there are lots of bunches of shiny purple fruit hanging from the huge tree in the compound of the ghost house. I love zambas and the way they stain my mouth and tongue deep violet. I can never get enough of them.

We pause outside the closed wooden gate to the ghost house before crawling through an opening in the hedge.

"Who's climbing up?"

Everyone looks in my direction.

"Let's toss for it," I say, but no one is listening. They all know I'm the best climber.

"Maybe now he is in that posh school, he's forgotten how to climb trees," Odush laughs.

"Fine then! I'll climb," I say and sneak closer to the tree.

I wrap my arms and legs around the zambarau tree's rough, gray trunk. I haul myself up, inch by strenuous inch. My eyes never leave the door to the white house below. Scary thoughts of ghosts flap through my head. Any minute now they will burst out, soar up, and drag me into the decrepit house.

Why did I even agree to the mad idea of climbing the tree? Odush and the others are safe on the ground and could race off, leaving me alone with the ghosts. I fight the urge to abandon my climb halfway, and then it is too late, because I'm already at the top.

When no ghosts rush out of the deserted house, I work my way to the sides where most of the fruits dangle from the smaller branches. Soon, Mose and the others are howling for fruit.

"To your left, a little higher to the left, get the juicy ones!" Mose shouts, and me, I'm as scared as hell. Surely, with so much noise, whatever is in the house below will be alerted.

When nothing happens, my confidence soars and I edge on higher, to where I know I shouldn't. I reach out for a mouthwatering bunch and suddenly the branch snaps, and I'm hurtling down, with leaves and branches and all manner of things whizzing past, scratching my arms, slapping at my face.

Something whacks my wrist hard, before I slam against the corrugated iron roof of the ghost house and onto the hard ground. I do not remember rising, or squeezing through the hole in the hedge, but now I'm on Desai Street running like demons are on my tail.

Dado is with me, but I can't see the others. I'm out of breath.

My sides and my arm feel like someone has beaten me with a blackboard ruler.

"Are you okay?" Dado asks.

I nod.

"We thought you were smashed to pieces," Odush says when we catch up with him and Mose at the overpass.

"I didn't know you could fall from so high up and not . . ."

"Aha! So you thought he was dead?" Dado presses. "Is that why you scampered off, like two scared rabbits? Or maybe you were scared of ghosts."

Mose looks down and sketches in the dust with his foot.

Odush averts his eyes.

"What if the ghost of the dead woman and her daughter got me?" I ask with a smile.

"When you landed on the roof, I saw someone peer out from the window of the ghost house," Odush says and we fall silent.

"By God, I saw someone at the window," he swears, and we exchange glances.

I don't say a thing but there is something bothering me too. From up in the zamba tree I saw some smoke waft out from the chimney of the ghost house. Why would smoke come out of a deserted house? I wonder. But my hand is aching so I don't give it that much thought.

"*Awooooooo!*" Dado presses his palm against his mouth and wails like he is a ghost, and then we are laughing and also screaming, "*Awooooooo!*"

"Anyway, ghosts don't scare me," Odush says, and we aren't surprised. The guy always finds his words only after the threat is gone.

He spits on the ground and rubs the back of his hand against his mouth like the loaders at the railway.

Taking up his dare, Mose spits and so does Dado.

I try to spit, but my mouth is sore and my spit comes out red. I run my tongue over a gash inside the wall of my mouth. My hand aches like hell.

We draw a line in the dust and stand behind it, to see who spits farthest. If it wasn't for the pain in my mouth I would be second. Only Dado can out-spit me. We spit and spit until our mouths are dry.

Dado wins, Odush sulks, and we go our separate ways.

CHAPTER NINE

* * *

LIKE A SHY TOAD that does not want to be seen, the railway dispensary squats behind the huge locomotive sheds. Parents often use it as a bogey to silence noisy kids. *I'll take you to the dispensary for an injection if you don't shut your mouth*, grown-ups will threaten them.

I'm with Mama in the dispensary waiting room. My left arm is swollen the size of a cassava tuber, and it feels like there is a fire under my skin. Anything that might reduce the pain is welcome.

Mama looks everywhere but at me. She does that when she is angry. Right now she is mad at me for breaking my arm yesterday and concealing it until today. She says I could easily have lost the arm.

There are other kids with their mothers in the waiting room. I don't see any fathers, just mothers and their coughing, crying babies. I guess fathers are at work, or they just don't like dispensaries.

The stench of disinfectant tickles my nostrils. It stings my eyes and settles at the back of my throat, never going away.

A nurse in white shouts "Next," and a mother rises with her

child, to disappear behind a door marked EXAMINATION ROOM. The rest of us slide our backsides against the wooden benches and inch closer. It must be the sliding that has worn the benches smooth and shiny.

THE DOCTOR WEARS A white lab coat with a name tag that says Dr. Jeevanje. He sits behind a big brown desk. A happy smile plays under his jet-black mustache. Even though I'm the one who is sick, he gestures Mama into the only empty chair, while I remain standing. He examines my arm, rings a bell on his desk, and a slim lady in white appears.

"I think he will need an X-ray of his left arm," he tells the lady, who ushers me through a side door and to the X-ray room.

"LUMUMBA, how did you break your arm?" The doctor raises the big black picture a nurse has handed him, against an overhead light. "Most probably playing football?" he says, not waiting for my response.

I nod.

"Don't let him fool you. The scoundrel fell from a tree while stealing people's fruits," Mama shoots me a warning look. "Imagine—at his age and being in Hill School, he still goes about climbing trees," Mama clucks.

"Aha! So you are in Hill School?" the doctor looks up. "I had a son there. He finished a couple of years ago. Does Mr. Bumbles still teach there?"

I nod.

"You must have been named after Patrice Lumumba? He was a great man. You know that, don't you?"

I nod again. How could I not know when Baba sings about this Lumumba guy, day in and day out? How the African continent lost one of its greatest sons to some people he calls "imperialists." And that the guy was from Congo, which has diamonds as big as a baby's fist and other precious metals sticking out from the ground, just waiting to be picked. How the imperialists had set their greedy eyes on the diamonds and since it was only this Lumumba guy standing between them and the diamonds, they had to kill him like a dog.

Africa's riches are her curse."You have a fracture, which will require a cast," Dr. Jeevanje says and rises from behind his desk. He is taller than I'd expected. He tells me how he broke his arm twice as a kid. He jokes about the plaster, says it will be one dirty mess when I return to have it removed in a month's time. It might even have lice on the inside.

Mama makes a laughing sound, but I know she is not really laughing. I can tell from the way she keeps blinking. Her eyelids snap up and down, like they are competing to see which one can move faster. She does that when she is really mad.

Dado's mum stops us near the pharmacy, to fuss over my broken hand. She has a spotless, white uniform.

Mama pretends to smile, grabs my good arm, and propels me away.

"Two tablets; twice a day," a short, fat, balding man says and hands us medicine at the pharmacy.

We step out into the sunlight and Mama storms ahead as though she has remembered some place she has to hurry to.

I follow from a safe distance.

MOSE TAPS MY CAST—*tock, tock, tock.* "Wish I could get one, then no one would mess with me."

"You'll have to break your arm if you want one."

"Must be painful?"

"Yah!"

"Is it really broken, or just a sprain?"

"Of course it's broken. They even took an X-ray."

"You mean the big, black pictures that show bones?"

I nod, and we lean on the Zephyr and stare ahead. Sometimes it feels great just staring.

A green grasshopper leaps out from the grass like something is after its life. It lands on the Zephyr's hood, slides to the ground, and vaults off into the browned grass. Lost in our thoughts, we do not move. I don't know what Mose is thinking, but me, it is about the time a big brown grasshopper landed on Njish's lap. She leaped off her seat and yelled so loud, Teacher Focus panicked and ran out of class. When he realized it was just an innocent hopper that had caused the ruckus, he ordered the entire class to stay in during break, as punishment. For days I could see the embarrassment on his face.

"Do you think Odush really saw a ghost in the white house?" Mose asks in a whisper.

"What do you think?"

"I don't know! But he looked scared before you and Dado caught up with us."

"Odush is always scared. He pretends to be tough but the guy is a wimp," I say.

A kite swoops downward then lifts off. Something white flutters under its wide wings as it glides away. What fun it would be, to be able to fly about like the kite and go anywhere that I please.

"Why are you smiling?" Mose says, and I ignore him.

A jet plane slices through the clouds. It leaves a long, fluffy, white tail in its wake. I once saw some jets from the waving bay of Embakasi Airport. Huge monsters, those jets, bigger and better than stupid trains. When the pilot turned on the turbines, I felt it right in my gut.

The plane is barely visible now. It floats on and on like it doesn't have a care in the world. Maybe it's arriving from some far-off place. Could be it's off to another country and the people in it are going away for good. Me, when I get into one of those, I will go and never come back. Then Mama can find some other backside to use her switch on.

A muzungu with the Peace Corps once told us that in their country parents get in trouble for caning children. They even get locked up in prison.

If they did that here, Mama would spend the rest of her life in prison.

CHAPTER TEN

✱ ✱ ✱

"WHY DON'T WE VISIT the deserted house on Desai Street at night," Dado says. "After all, it is the time ghosts come out to haunt." He grins.

"Are you crazy? You think I'm going to risk my neck in that eerie place at night? It's scary enough during the day. There's no way I'm going there at night," Odush shakes his head.

"If we want to find out whether there really are ghosts in that house, we have to go there after dark," Dado insists, and me, I'm wondering whether it's a good idea. What would Mama say if she heard I'd gone to that evil house at night?

"Don't you think the ghosts will have an advantage over us in the dark? At least during the day we'll be able to see them in good time and run if we have to," Mose laughs.

"And how would you know that ghosts see better at night?" I ask.

"I don't know what it was I saw behind the window of the abandoned house the day you fell from the tree, but I swear, something moved," Odush repeats what he told us before. "I'm not going anywhere near it at night. You people can tell me what's in it if you come out alive."

"And how are we supposed to get out of our houses at night without our parents knowing?" I ask. "My mother is still mad at me for climbing that tree and breaking my arm."

"We could do it on Friday after the open-air film is over. That way no one would know we are planning on going there," Dado suggests.

"Count me out," Odush says with finality. "Do you people even know what a ghost can do to you? It can enter your body and turn you into one of them."

"We don't even know if there are ghosts in that house," Dado says. "And even if there are, I thought you said you weren't afraid of ghosts?" He eyeballs Odush.

"That was then and this is now. And also that was during the day. Now you are suggesting we go at night."

"Maybe we should toss on whether to go. Heads we go, tails we don't." Mose pulls out a ten-cent coin, and I'm not surprised because he is always betting over everything. He tosses the coin in the air and clamps it in his fist as it falls.

Odush shouts, "tails," but it's heads.

"So Film Friday it will be," Dado says. "That's only two days away. I'll bring a flashlight along."

"I'll bring a rosary and a crucifix to scare the ghosts. I read somewhere they can't stand religious stuff," Mose says.

"And Odush can bring some of that holy water the Riswa people who worship and beat drums in their houses sprinkle on themselves," Dado laughs and we all join in.

"Me, I'll be between Mose and Odush the whole time, so the ghosts don't get me. And if they get close, I'll hammer them with this." I raise my left arm in its cast and laugh.

"Wait until those ghosts enter your body, then you will wish you had sprinkled some holy water on yourself," Odush wags a forefinger at me.

IT'S FRIDAY EVENING and the film corporation truck is already parked at the edge of the estate playfield near the social hall. Mama sent me to Mama Nandwa's kiosk for a packet of milk, but I've decided to stop and watch the adverts.

A fat lady in a neat white apron fills the big white cinema screen. She scoops large portions of cooking fat into a frying pan. "*Pika kwa Kimbo. Pika kwa Kimbo,*" she sings out.

Her wide smile never fades as she flips crisp brown chapatis. When the Ambi lady begins to rub cream on her long legs, I suddenly remember the milk Mama sent me to buy, and I'm off like Kipchoge Keino. That's the Kenyan who won gold medals at the Olympics. He would sometimes lap the other athletes and you would think they were winning when the truth was that he was a whole lap ahead of them.

"ANYONE WHO LEAVES without helping with the dishes better find their own house to come back to," Mama says, after we've had our supper.

She is always saying weird things. Other times she says that if there was a market where children were sold, she would sell us all at half price. I try to picture a big market where sweaty men drag screaming kids along, instead of sacks of cabbages and potatoes, and shout out, "*Fifty shillings for two healthy boys; a good bargain*," and buyers make offers.

Awino's head is buried inside her Safari book. She pretends to concentrate on it, but me, I know she is spying on us. She will inform Mama the minute she sees us leave. As if it will add any sugar to her tea.

Deno presses a finger to his lips to gesture for her silence and she nods. Deno is also going to the film and Awino always listens to him.

Apondi is washing dishes and singing:

"*Good morning Mr. Ooko,*

I come and see your daughter."

"You want to make her angry?" Deno says when I start to laugh.

"No!"

"Apondi, can we leave?"

Apondi just continues singing.

"Please!"

Still nothing!

"Maybe we should just go," I whisper to Deno.

"So what if you go? You are not helping anyone with anything. You think those stupid films you are rushing to see will help you in your exams? No one will ask you about people kicking and punching each other, or about mannerless people kissing each other. Go! I don't care," Apondi shouts, and we are off like the house is on fire.

I SQUEEZE THROUGH the crowd in the playfield, drawing curses each time I step on someone's foot. All the faces look the same in the moonlight. A shrill sound pierces the night, and I know it is Dado whistling. I shove two fingers into my mouth to let out a response. A couple more whistle blasts and I trace my three friends.

"What's with you, man? You almost missed the Coming-Soons," Mose says as I flop down by his side.

A Chinese man wearing all black appears on the screen. Without warning, another in blue pajama-like trousers leaps into his path.

"You killed my brother," the man in blue screams and punches out as the other blocks the punches. His ponytail bobs up and down. They kick, chop, and punch like they are dancing. As one advances, the other retreats. They make sounds like "ugh" and "agh." Their kicks slice through wooden poles, and the punches leave cracks in the walls. In no time they are flying around and around, like the overhead fans at the railway platform.

Mose kicks out in his excitement.

The guy in black runs off with the other in hot pursuit. They run with brief, jerky steps.

"Just watch the action that follows," Mose says and elbows me. "I'll bet you Chang Sing beats Wang Yu," he says, but the two men just stare each other out, then turn and walk away.

"Ahhh!" Mose sighs in disappointment.

"Who doesn't know that you can't chop through logs with your bare hands? These guys don't even know how to fake things. They fly about like they are dancing. No one gets hurt, no one wins, and there's no story. Their faces are blank. They don't smile, laugh, or cry. They just go on and on and on," Dado says.

"Did you bring a flashlight?" I ask Dado, just to remind everyone we will be going to the ghost house.

"Of course I did."

"And you, Mose, your rosary?"

"Oh! Yes."

"And, Odush, did you bring your holy water?" I ask, and we all laugh.

"I'll sprinkle it on you right here and now if you don't shut up."

After a long wait the main feature of the film begins. A man in the film corporation truck runs a commentary in his shrill voice. Most of the time he exaggerates, but we love the way he does it. His voice rises and falls, like he is singing:

"Here comes Otero on horseback, *Kukuru, kakara; Kukuru, kakara*," the man rhymes out the sound of horse hooves against the ground. "Haiya! Now you will see Otero avenge the deaths of his people. If I were those thugs, I would fly like the wind, before Otero arrives," he warns, as if the actors can hear what he is saying.

Not long after, the lead actor gets off his big brown horse. His blue eyes are as still as marbles. He pulls off his hat, turns his back to us, and is about to enter a place that has the word SALOON on a sign above it, when three thugs appear.

"Haiya!" the commentator exclaims, and everyone goes silent.

Faster than the eyes can see, the lead actor draws out his guns and shoots—*gushungya, gushungya, gushungya.*

When the dust settles, the bad guys are sprawled on the ground and we all break out in cheers as he holsters his smoking guns.

"You can't shoot three people so fast," Dado says. "Do they think we're stupid?"

"It's only a film, man!" Odush groans.

"Why don't they show us things that are real? Even the blood isn't real. I'm sure it's tomato sauce."

"Since when do you know anything about acting? Just shut your big mouth and watch," Odush says.

"Who doesn't know that the guns they use are fake? They're the kind they use to start races."

"Did you expect them to kill each other for real with real guns? Just shut up and watch the film."

"Why can't they show us wildlife films with African actors, instead of these ufala things."

"Look! One of those guys is not dead. I just saw him move," Odush says, and we all focus back on the screen.

Sure enough, one of the bad guys slowly rises and slips out a tiny gun from his jacket. We shout out warnings to the lead actor, who ignores us and continues to walk away. With barely seconds to spare, he turns and shoots the bad guy between the eyes, driving him back down.

Everyone claps and cheers as the hero mounts his horse.

"At least they have Black people in wildlife films," Dado says as the lead actor rides off into the sunset.

"Even those wildlife films are made by white people. They only allow a few Black people to play ufala roles of cooks and watchmen," Odush says. "That's the way things are and you can't change it, so let's just watch the film."

"I once saw a film where all the actors were Asians, including the lead, and they were speaking in their language and singing their own songs," Mose says. "If we want to have films where we aren't cooks and watchmen we must make our own. Me, I'm going to be an actor."

"Aren't you the one who is always laughing at Njish when she plays Mary in the school play?" I say.

"That's different. I'm not talking about ufala school plays, where they dress up like dolls to sing. I want to be in films where I can punch people and shoot them dead. And what's with Njish acting as the mother of Jesus when she is Black and the mother of Jesus was white?"

"That's only in the books and films where they show Jesus and everyone as white, but it's not true."

"So, now Jesus wasn't white?"

"He could have been any color."

"You mean, like black?" Mose sniggers.

"Maybe even brown, like an Asian."

"He could have been an Arab," Dado says.

"But Arabs are Muslims. You want to say Jesus was a Muslim?"

"No one was talking to you," Dado glowers at Odush.

"And how are you going to act as Otero or the Chinese guy in pajamas when you are Black?" Odush asks Mose.

"They'll dress him up in pajamas and give him one of those cook or watchman roles," Dado says and laughs.

The film is over, but the projector whirs on. The names of everyone who did something in the film appear on the screen. There are soundmen, costume designers, and lots of other people. The playfield empties, but we hang around the film truck and watch them roll up the cables, bring down the screen. They pack the film reels in flat, round, silver cans and stack them in a wooden box. The corporation man hands us sweets before they all drive off.

Then we head for the railway overpass and on to Desai Street. The only sound is that of our feet against the asphalt, because none of us is talking.

We stop at the spot where we went through the hedge the last time we visited the ghost house. At least today we are not climbing any trees, so I don't have to go in first.

"You have your magic water to protect you from ghosts, so you go first," I tell Odush.

"It's you who said you don't believe in ghosts, so you go first," he moves away from the hole in the hedge.

We are still arguing in whispers when Dado drops to his knees and crawls through. I follow closely and Mose is right behind me. Odush with his holy water follows last.

"Shhh," Dado cautions.

"It's cold out here," Odush whispers.

"And where is that whistling sound coming from?" Mose's hand touches my back, and I almost jump with fright.

"That's the wind blowing through the leaves above. Now, if we want to find out what's in there, we better shut up," Dado warns.

"I don't think it was a good idea to come here and mess with dead people's spirits," Odush laments. "And look at the way the moon is dancing between the dark clouds above. Evil spirits are active when the moon does that."

"Shhh. If you didn't want to come, you should have stayed at home," Dado says, but now I'm also scared.

Images of a film we watched with Deno at Cameo Cinema, where some archaeologists opened up the tomb of an Egyptian pharaoh, flash through my mind. Tall mummies wound in stained bandages, their arms extended as they pursued the archaeologists who had disturbed their rest. Their eerie screams fill my ears.

"I think we should just leave, before something happens to us," Mose's whisper jolts me back to the present and, at that very moment, a creaking sound comes from the direction of the front door to the house, causing us to freeze.

A bright light flashes on and off, revealing a silhouette from behind one of the windows. However, it is the eerie, grinding sound from somewhere in the dark compound that spurs us to action and then we are off, fighting to get away from the scary place.

Odush is first out through the hole in the hedge. I bump into Mose as I try to squeeze through and we are stuck there for a while, and then I'm out on the deserted road, running. For the second time we are fleeing from the ghost house, only this time it is dark.

CHAPTER ELEVEN

✳ ✳ ✳

"WHAT'S ALL THAT NOISE ABOUT? Can't you see your father is trying to sleep? And all you can do is chatter away like monkeys," Mama shouts out from the kitchen.

We are in the living room. I'm supposed to be doing my homework, but I have a comic book in between the pages of my history textbook. Mama is preparing supper.

"It's Lumush who's scaring me," Awino says in her put-on girly tone.

"No! It's Awino who is going on and on about ghosts," I say.

"If I hear another word about ghosts, I will whack your bottom sore, Lumush, do you hear me? I don't know what it is they teach you in that Hill School. And don't forget that yesterday you crept back into this house at midnight, two hours after your brother returned from watching the open-air film. You think I didn't hear him open the door for you? You think I'm deaf? Don't you even think for a minute that because you have that dirty cast on your arm I will not be able to punish you. After all, you broke your arm stealing fruits," Mama goes on and on and you would think that

I robbed a bank. Mama is always connecting things, so that little things you have done over a long time become one huge thing and then she has a reason to punish you.

"BABA, do you think ghosts exist? Do you think the white house on Desai Street is haunted?" I ask, after we have eaten our supper.

"You mean the house that belonged to Mr. Swiney? The man they found dead in his car after his wife and child died? Ghosts are just one of the names we give to things we can't explain. There's a logical explanation to everything. One just has to find it," Baba says.

CHAPTER TWELVE

* * *

I RETURN FROM SCHOOL one evening to find Uncle Owuoth in our living room.

"How was school?" he asks in his throaty voice, which Mama says is because of too much alcohol.

"Fine," I say.

"I can see you no longer have your cast. How does your hand feel?"

"Fine," I lift my arm up. "I had it removed yesterday."

"Awino tells me you broke it at a haunted house?"

I nod and move a little closer. I know Uncle Owuoth has experience with lots of things and he might know something about haunted houses and ghosts.

"Spirits do exist," Uncle does not wait for me to ask. "Once when I was in Mombasa I met a woman dressed in one of those black buibuis they love at the coast. She had a veil and her voice was as sweet as honey fresh from a hive. But it was the way she walked that made me suspicious. I glanced down under the hem of her buibui and where there should have been feet, there were hooves. Hooves like you see on cows and goats." Uncle Owuoth raises his hand to his mouth as though he is living the moment all over again. "Her identity having been revealed, she melted away into the dark night. Oh, yes, ghosts and other spirits exist. At the coast they call them jinns."

Uncle Owuoth is Baba's real, elder brother, so Baba has to respect him, even when he gets drunk and makes a fool of himself by dancing and throwing up all over the living room floor. When he does that, Mama gives him one of those looks that say, *Were it not for your brother, I would break your head with my rolling pin*, and trust me, she would. But he is Baba's elder brother, so everyone must respect him. After all, he paid Baba's school fees.

Uncle Owuoth shows up from shaggs at the end of the month for what Mama calls "handouts." Even after he has received the handouts he is in no hurry to leave. He spends the afternoon drinking at Maskani, which is what people call Apima's drinking den. Mama sends Apondi to go check if he is spending Baba's "hard-earned money" on women with big backsides and painted lips. Apondi never gets past Mwachuma's scrapyard before returning to lie that he is already drunk and is buying drinks for anyone who so much as flashes a smile at him. She does that because it is what Mama expects her to say.

Uncle once worked at Mombasa's port. People would trip over each other to buy him a bottle of Allsopps, which was understandable. Who didn't want to be a friend of the first African crane operator? Yes, Uncle claims he was the first African to learn how to operate a crane at the port. It was a honor just to be seen with him. But that was before he married a second wife and began to drink the local mnazi brew. Soon enough he lost his job.

Uncle Owuoth has lots of stories of the places he's been to and the things he's done. He has been a sailor, a musician, a magician, and even a smuggler. He doesn't talk about the part of being a smuggler when Baba is around. He once even joined a seminary to be a priest, but cut short his studies when he realized that all those hypocrites studying to be priests were nothing but whiskey-drinking womanizers.

Uncle's stories always begin with, "When I was . . ." and are all about things that happened a long time ago, when he was still "a Somebody." He has been to Congo, Zanzibar, Pemba, and even Sri Lanka, where he says the people are blacker than him. He can play a guitar and blow a saxophone, and once played in a club called Casablanca on the coast. He was also a damn good footballer.

Baba just smiles and says nothing when Uncle recounts his escapades. Mama, on the other hand, says that the only game Uncle plays is at Apima's with Baba's money.

IT'S SUNDAY NIGHT. Baba's Grundig record player is playing a song called "Lek" by Kabaselleh. He croons out how a dream led him from his home in Ujimbe to a place he had never been to before. He sings of finding ten sacks full of hundred-shilling notes, and while hauling the loot back, he awakens to the rude reality; it is only a dream.

Though his foot is tapping to the beat, Baba is not humming along. I know he loves Kabaselleh and swears the guy sings better than Jim Reeves. That's the dead musician who sang *"This world is not my home, I'm just passing through. . . ."* Such a compliment coming from Baba is no small thing, because he loves Jim Reeves.

Today, Baba's head is buried behind his *Standard* newspaper. He is reading about how Idi Amin expelled the muhindis from Uganda. He starts to read out loud:

"They were not making the journey of their own volition. Their crinkled saris, crumpled dhoti-pants and Punjabi suits attested to it. The overnight bags tightly clutched to their sides, was proof of it. The dark rings under their eyes showed they had barely slept. Who sleeps when they have only ninety days to leave their homes and country for unknown destinations?"

Baba looks up, clucks his tongue, and continues:

"Experienced in trade and industry, these forlorn men and women had been the drivers of the economy of the country they had been forced out of. Who would have predicted the very same railway their forebears had broken their backs for, and lost their lives building, some three generations ago, would be the very same one transporting them to uncertain futures."

"Amin is mad to chase away the Asians," Baba says and folds his newspaper.

"Serves them right for living cloistered lives and keeping to themselves," says Uncle Owuoth.

"Uganda's economy is finished," Baba says.

Mama too is in the living room, but she doesn't say a word. She never says anything when Uncle Owuoth is around. It's only after he is gone that she will talk about him. Even though Uncle Owuoth only has six children, Mama will ask why he would have a dozen children when he has no job. She's always exaggerating like that. Other times she will blame Baba for Uncle's wayward behavior. But now that Uncle is in the living room, she is silent.

"Everything that works belongs to the Asians. The economy will certainly collapse."

Baba always talks about this economy thing, and how it can grow or collapse. It seems it is the Asians who know how to grow it.

"They are nothing but cheating dukawalas who send all their profits back home," Uncle says.

"Which home? Most of them were born in Uganda."

Uncle does not respond, but Baba goes on about a Mr. D'souza, who speaks better Kiswahili than most Africans. "The man often jokes about how his people find themselves between the insensitive mortar of the whites and the angry pestle of the Black Africans, how they have lived their lives dodging the blows that have never ceased."

Uncle remains quiet.

"There was this Asian man called Abdul Khan. People called him Simba Mbili. He was a sub-permanent railway inspector, who rode a small pump trolley along the railway line to ensure that the line was undamaged and secure. One time his party was attacked by a pride of lions, and he shot them down one after the other until only two remained. By then he had only one bullet in his rifle. Taking careful aim, Abdul shot the lead lion and the bullet went clean through its body and lodged into the head of the other, killing them both. That's how he got the name Simba Mbili."

"I've heard the story before. It doesn't mean it is true."

"That's not the point."

"Then what is the point?"

"The point is one can't ignore the massive contribution the Asians have made toward the building of the railway and the two countries it traverses. Did you also know that Kenya's own motto, the word "Harambee," was borrowed from them? It was their rallying call while building the railway."

This time Uncle seems surprised, but his brow is now bunched. It is obvious he is only listening because he has to. If it were not for the money Baba dishes out to him at the end of every month, he'd probably walk away.

"IDI AMIN IS A MADMAN," Mama says after Uncle Owuoth has retired to bed and she is alone with Baba. "The scoundrel sent all those Asians away because they would not allow him to marry one of their daughters."

"That's cheap propaganda," Baba says.

"What of the stories of trucks dumping helpless, disabled people into the lake? Is that also propaganda? And you, where are your manners sitting there listening to grown-up talk?" Mama turns in my direction, and I'm off like a bat from the rafters of Grandpa's house in shaggs.

THE NEXT EVENING, Uncle Owuoth eats his supper and retires to bed early. Baba has yet to get his salary, so Uncle will be around for a while.

"Shhh!" Baba calls for silence and adjusts the volume of his Grundig two-in-one radio. The nine o'clock obituary announcements are on:

"*We regret to announce the deaths of . . .*" The radio announcer drones on in his sad tone. He reels off the names of dead people and their close relatives. Some are in other countries in far-off lands. He mentions Germany, the USA, England, France, and some places I've never even heard of. In-laws and other not-too-close relatives are mentioned last. Baba's eyes are pinched and his lips pressed together in concentration.

The announcements are over. Baba usually knows one or two of the dead people or their relatives, and he'll ramble on about how they were schoolmates, or how they married from the same place. He often says, the older you get, the more friends and relatives you have, some through marriage and others through work. Today, Baba hasn't heard a name he knows.

BABA RETURNS HOME from work one evening and slaps his *Standard* newspaper hard on the table. There is a picture of one of his workmates on the front page. The man was pulled out of a train in

Uganda and was whipped by Amin's soldiers. He is lucky he didn't get shot because that's what they do to people they disagree with. No one knows exactly what happened. Whatever it was, the man was beaten up and has awful, angry welts on his back.

From then on, Idi Amin becomes Baba's enemy.

But Amin doesn't know Baba, and even if he did he wouldn't care less. He is busy doing more important things, like naming himself Conqueror of the British Empire, or claiming parts of Kenya. His smiling face is always in the papers. He is a field marshal, a boxer, a champion swimmer, and a musician. He tries his hand at rallying. His smart uniform is always full of medals, most of which he awarded himself. But medals or no medals, the man looks huge and fearsome. He even makes white people carry him on their shoulders. He looks like he could fight a war on his own, and win.

"AND WHAT DO YOU EXPECT of Amin? I've heard that the crazy guy even keeps human hearts in his fridge and eats human liver for breakfast," Mose says, after I tell him that Amin's soldiers whipped Baba's friend. It's Saturday morning, and I'm with Mose in our courtyard watching Deno's pigeons flap about under the awning of our house. They shoot up into the clear sky, their wings beating—*tapa, tapa, tapa*, before they swoop back into a wooden box that Deno built.

"There is nothing wrong with Amin. It's the Asians that are a problem. They carry away all their profits," I echo what I heard Uncle Owuoth say.

"So now Amin is a hero?"

"Of course he is a hero! His only mistake is chasing away the Asians," I say and wonder if what I've said even makes sense.

"Make sure you clean the pigeon house. Mum has been complaining about the foul smell," Deno says, appearing from nowhere before sauntering off to the Railway Club to play football.

Deno has six pigeons. One is gray, two are brown, and the rest are white. I can never tell the white ones apart. The scraping noise they make from inside their box is irritating, but their cooing is cool.

"Better tap the box with this before you shove your hand in there," I hand Mose a broom handle .

"Why?"

"We once found a shiny snake in there," I say, and Mose almost falls off the metal garbage bin he is perched on.

He eyes the box for a long time, then bangs its sides.

I climb up next to him to scrape the bird droppings, before we head for the old Zephyr.

"My father says the Asians have contributed greatly to this country," I slide up on the hood of the Zephyr. "If you expel them like Amin did in Uganda, the economy would collapse, and the factories would shut down, and the whole country would be in trouble," I say, even though I'm not sure why that would happen.

"I think they should stay. I love their laddus, samosas, and the way they play cricket," Mose strikes a batting pose and hits an imaginary ball.

"Those Asians built the railway and this here is their country." I tilt my head like Baba does when he is saying something important.

"But why do they always keep to themselves like they have another country of their own, right here?"

"In Hill School they mix pretty well. There is this tall boy in our class called Jaswant Singh, who can do crazy things with a cricket ball," I say and immediately regret it because I should know better than to discuss Hill School stuff with Mose or the others.

"That's just school. If he invited you home, their guard would probably never let you past the gate. And why do the guards and gardeners get angrier than their Asian employers?"

"They could get sacked if they didn't get angry."

"Who employs anyone just to get angry? If I was one of them I would make angry faces, but I would never be angry."

"That's why you will never be a guard."

"Who says I can't be an angry guard or gardener? Look at my angry guard face," Mose says and shuts his eyes and mouth so tight he looks like a constipated baby trying to poop. "Now it's your turn to be an angry gardener," he says.

I too try to pull an angry gardener face, but it doesn't come out right because Mose is laughing.

CHAPTER THIRTEEN

* * *

"THE DAY YOU FOOLS GET killed by ghosts is the day you will know not to joke with evil spirits," Apondi wags her forefinger at me. "Don't you know that house is haunted? If you knew the kind of sounds I've heard coming from that satanic house you would never go near it. But you idiots have to go there. And at night too. How foolish can you be?"

I look into Awino's eyes and she looks away.

"Who cheated you that we went anywhere near the ghost house? I'd be too scared to go anywhere near it at night," I pretend, even though I already know who snitched on us. It has to be Mose who told his sister, Ciiru, who then told her friend Awino, who in turn told Apondi. Ciiru and Awino are best friends.

"Do you know what ghosts do to people who disturb their rest? They enter your mind and scramble it so that you become mad," Apondi rolls her eyes and twists her mouth. "Do you want to start picking garbage? Well, that is exactly what will happen to you and your stupid friends if you don't watch out," Apondi places her forefinger on her head.

"I know it is Awino who told you all that and it's a lie."

"Told me what? Told me that you are stubborn and an idiot? Awino doesn't have to tell me anything, I can figure out things for myself. So don't go blaming your little sister over things she knows nothing about." Apondi turns to Awino who looks at a spot on the wall, pretending she doesn't know what we are talking about. "Wait until your mother finds out, then you will be in real trouble," Apondi storms away.

"SO YOU HAD TO GO and tell Ciiru about our visit to the ghost house," I confront Mose later in the day.

"I never told anyone anything." He combs the ground with his eyes, draws a map on the ground with his feet.

"Didn't you know that Ciiru would tell Awino who would tell Apondi, and then the whole estate would know?"

Mose stays silent.

"If Apondi knows, then everyone including my mum will know. Wait until I tell Dado and Odush that you can't keep your mouth shut." I look in the direction of Dado, who has just appeared at the edge of Block 6 and is heading in our direction.

"Please don't tell Dado. Ciiru promised she wouldn't tell anyone and I believed her."

"So now you admit telling Ciiru?"

"I didn't tell anyone anything."

"Which is it? Did you tell her or didn't you?"

Mose's eyes shift to Dado, who has reached where we are standing. He doesn't say another word.

"You look like you've just seen a ghost." Dado punches Mose on the arm.

Mose shoots me a pleading look.

I ignore him.

CHAPTER FOURTEEN

✳ ✳ ✳

SIX IN THE MORNING, the railway siren lets out a sad wail. A locomotive's head rises out from the morning fog. *Tidingtadang, tidingtadang*, it rhymes. Its steel wheels crunch against the metal tracks. Like a dancer gyrating to rumba music, the train sways this way and that way with silver bogies on its tail. Shortly after, it will resume its dance out of the yard, past Railway Estate and on to the coast in Mombasa.

The bogies are full of coffee from Uganda. Baba speaks of Uganda with nostalgia. He once worked there, in Jinja, which he says is the source of the Nile. He says they grow lots of coffee in Uganda and people call it "black gold."

Kids in the estate never miss out on an opportunity to wave at trains. Running along the metal barriers that fence off the rail tracks, they wave at the goods train as though the goods will come alive and wave back.

Today is different though. Today is the first Saturday of the month and the sprayers are expected. So most mothers have locked their kids indoors.

The sun is already peeping in between Mama's orange blinds, when I finally catch a glimpse of one of the sprayers in green overalls. His back is arched from the weight of the spray tank he carries. A second man joins him and a third. They resemble space invaders about to launch an attack, and anything silly enough to cross their path will die.

The sprayers fan out to spray the grass, the trees, hedges, and gutters. They open manholes and spray into the sewers below. I slip out to watch them spray under the rusted Zephyr. The short frangipani trees at the back of our block aren't spared. One of the men clambers onto a garbage bin to spray the sparsely leaved branches. Their mouths and noses are covered with handkerchiefs. Done with the spraying, they melt away just as they came. They'll be back, the first Saturday of the next month.

For days after the spraying, the gutters will shimmer with oily color and everything will smell funny. Anything that as much as sips the gutter water will end up dead. Even birds daft enough to drink from it will die and their blue bellies will swell and burst open like ripe pomegranates. Their skinny legs will point skyward.

"It's for the mosquitoes and bugs. Those tiny mosquitoes can kill a grown man. They once stood up to the imperialists. Armed only with their malaria they successfully defended some parts of the land from the colonialists. We should have a day set aside in honor of the scrawny mosquitoes for a job well done. We could even honor them on National days, instead of dishing out medals to big-bellied politicians," Baba guffaws.

Defenders or not, I hate mosquitoes. They go *ndiiiiiiiiiiii*, around your ears, and you slap out, *pap*, but the bloodsuckers are gone. Then the shivering, sweating, and throwing up begins, and Mama gives you foul-tasting Malariaquin tablets with a spindly legged mosquito drawn on the packet, which makes you throw up even more.

But it's the itching I hate the most. Once you have swallowed the malaria tablets you itch and scratch like Mwachuma's mongrel, Tarzan, who is always leashed in his scrapyard.

Tumbo is next. He barges into our living room without knocking. He is one of the estate overseers and thinks he owns the estate. He is dressed in stiff khaki shorts and over-polished black shoes. He has a clipboard in his hand. A sharpened pencil sticks out from behind his ear. His starched shorts and shirt make him look like an overgrown scout. I can almost picture him snapping his heels, lifting two fingers, and reciting the scout's code: *On my honor I will do my best to do my duty to God and my country . . .*

Tumbo's mission is to confirm that our quarters are maintained in a "liveable" condition, whatever that means. I wonder whether he has ever inspected the haunted house on Desai Street, which is technically also a railway house.

He places his Vaselined hands against his hips and pushes his big stomach forward. Just looking at him makes me laugh because "Tumbo" means stomach in Kiswahili. He pulls the pencil from behind his ear and uses it to drum on his clipboard. He eyes me, and I look away because kids aren't supposed to look grown-ups in the eye. At least, that's what Mama says.

Apondi is in our courtyard. She is singing and rinsing a huge green blanket. She sticks it between her thighs and twists the other end until you think it can't twist any more and will snap in two. She wipes her brow with the back of her hands. Soapsuds stick to her face.

Tumbo is frozen to the spot, his eyes glued on Apondi, who tosses the blanket into a bucket of clear water and turns her attention to the pile of bedsheets at her feet.

Tumbo has moved to a corner of our courtyard. He uses his pencil to poke at a mattress laid out to air. He sniffs at it the way strays would sniff the hindquarters of Mose's dog, Fanta, before it drank the gutter water after spraying and died. Tumbo's eyes light up as he scribbles on his clipboard.

Sniff. Scribble. Sniff. Scribble.

Apondi straightens from her washing, pushes past Tumbo, and flips my mattress over.

Tumbo steps back to scribble something on his board. He throws furtive glances over his shoulders. His machete-stiff, starched shorts stick out like they could slice through anything they come in contact with.

"Why don't you get out of here? Go find your hopeless friends near that old car," Apondi scolds me.

I stick out my tongue at her. I know she is saying that so I can get in trouble with Mama. Apondi would be the first one to report to Mama that I went out immediately after the spraying. I retreat to a corner from where I can watch Tumbo.

TUMBO EDGES CLOSE. He pauses to examine the courtyard wall. He uses his pen to scrape it in places where it has greened with mold. From up close, his hair is brown. He must have dyed it with Kanta. The stuff keeps hair black for a while before it turns copper brown, like the hair of the man who sells bedsheets and pillowcases. Mama always swears not to buy anything from him, but once he roars in on his white Vespa, she can't help buying one thing or the other. She pays him in installments. Sometimes they get into an argument, when she delays in paying.

Mama uses Kanta on Baba's hair. Once a month, she mixes the stuff with water in a metal dish, runs it through Baba's hair using a toothbrush. Some of it runs down the nape of his neck, leaving a black trail, which she wipes off with a wet cloth. The hair stays jet-black for a week, before coppering.

Tumbo turns to catch me watching him. He knows it's his dyed hair I'm staring at. He screws his face, brushes past, heads for the next house.

He will be back with the sprayers, the next first Saturday of the month, and most activities in the estate will again grind to a halt. Though no one in the estate says it, I think they could do without the sprayers and overseers. At least I'm sure the kids would.

CHAPTER FIFTEEN

*** * ***

I FIRST LEARN OF the trip to St. Josephs from Roba, the other boy from Railway Estate. He often avoids me at Hill School, so when he walks up to me after lunch and flashes me a wide smile, I know there is something he wants from me.

"There is a trip for the debating club to St. Josephs next week, and Bumbles says it would be practical for one of us to lead the group because we were once students there."

I'm surprised. I'm not even a member of the debating club. But I'm interested in seeing where this is going, so I play along.

"That would be fun. But since you have been here longer than me, I propose you lead them," I smile.

"I was thinking you should go. You were popular at St. Josephs and would be able to make things work. That's what I told Bumbles, and he agrees with me," Roba averts his eyes and cracks his knuckles.

"So Bumbles also knows I was popular at St. Josephs?"

"I told him."

Did you also tell him that most of the students at St. Josephs think

Hill School is full of snobs who think too highly of themselves, I think to myself, but I don't say it. Instead, I tell Roba that I think he is popular enough to lead the gentlemen of Hill School, and then I walk away.

BUMBLES ASKS ME to remain behind after last class, and I know exactly why.

"You've settled in pretty well here at Hill School," he struggles to put on a smile and gestures me to a seat next to him. "The truth is I never thought you would, but you've proved me wrong, I must say," he grins.

I know where you are going. Just get on with it, I say in my head. But for him, I nod and smile.

"I admit there were times I was a bit harsh with you, but it was with the best intentions in mind."

Best intentions indeed. I don't consider suspecting me of stealing Kazungu's money without a shred of evidence to have been well-intentioned, I think but again do not say it. Instead I nod.

"But all that is behind us and I'm sure going forward, we will have a fruitful relationship," he sticks out his fleshy hand and places the other over my shoulder.

I stretch out my hand and it is immediately swallowed in his. Only then does he make his request.

"You must know by now that the debating club will be visiting your old school. Though you are not a member of the club, I was wondering whether you would agree to come along?" Bumbles lets out his brightest smile yet, and I am wondering how he would react if I said no to his face. But that would be insubordination and it would earn me a demerit on my conduct card.

So again I nod.

"Then that's settled," his smile vanishes and is replaced by a familiar frown. "We will work out the details at a later date," he rises and glides away.

FOR THE FEW DAYS BEFORE the trip to St. Josephs, Bumbles is full of smiles. "You all know that we will be paying a visit to our friends at . . . , what's the name of your former school, Lumumba?" Bumbles addresses me by name, which is unusual.

"St. Josephs," I mumble.

"Yes, that's it. On Thursday the debating club will be visiting St. Josephs, and Lumumba has been kind enough to agree to come with us," Bumbles smiles. "Unfortunately our visit to the same school last year was not very successful. However, this time, with Lumumba around, I know things will be different as he is familiar with the terrain, so to speak," he says.

Wow! It's amazing. In less than a minute, Bumbles has referred to me by name more times than he has done the entire period I have been in Hill School. He always refers to me as *you over there.* The man really needs this trip to succeed.

ON THURSDAY, after morning parade, we pile into the school bus and wait for Steven, the driver, to fire its engine.

Roba chooses to sit next to me in the bus, and attempts to strike up a conversation that doesn't go well. After a while he stares ahead in silence.

When we arrive at St. Josephs, Cleophas, the bell ringer and guard, waves our bus past the school's crooked red gate and on to the dusty drive, then Steven kills the engine.

"Lumumba will now lead us out," Bumbles says.

My heart is racing when I step off the bus. Maybe I should go down on my knees and kiss the ground. But that would be ridiculous. Worse still, I'm sure it would get me in trouble. Imagine me, on my knees, my lips on the dusty ground—Bumbles would think I was a traitor. And if Dado or Mose got to know about it they would have something to laugh about for the remainder of the school term.

I direct my classmates toward the St. Josephs school hall where the debate is to take place.

Unlike the airy, neat, wood-tiled hall at Hill School, the St. Josephs hall has cracks in the floor. In some parts it even has holes. The whole place is damp from water seeping into the walls when it rains, and the white paint has turned gray and peeled off in patches. A blend of nostalgia and shame swamps me and I fight the urge to make excuses over the state of things.

I do not need to look into Bumbles's eyes or the faces of my classmates to know what they think about my old school. But one thing is clear: my heart is still here at St. Josephs.

I mount the podium to introduce the students of both schools. I am about to begin when I catch a glance of Mose, Odush, and Dado. None of them are in the debating club, but they're in the audience. Dado sniggers, but one look from Teacher Focus and he turns his snigger into a cough.

Next to mount the rickety wooden podium is Njish. She says a short prayer and introduces the topic of debate: *Money is the root of all evil.*

Once the debate begins, the smudged walls, broken windows, and dilapidated state of St. Josephs are all forgotten as the debaters try to best each other.

Hill School's star debater, Kazungu, opens his mouth to speak but his words get stuck somewhere between his mouth and his bobbing Adam's apple. Bumbles's face turns so red, you would think he has a fire burning in his head and any minute there will be smoke spewing out from his ears.

Teacher Focus smiles. His face brightens with every passing minute.

Bumbles coughs to clear his throat. He pulls out a white hankie to wipe his face. It is only when Lillian takes to the podium that he flashes a weak smile.

The frown on Njish's face when I clap for Lillian's delivery, done in a crisp clear tone, freezes me. From then on Njish's eyes dart from Lillian on the podium to me.

The Hill School side erupts into applause as Lillian descends from the podium.

Njish dares me with her eyes, so I don't clap.

RAILWAY ESTATE IS just behind St. Josephs. It makes little sense for me to go all the way back to Hill School after the debate, just to walk back down the hill to the estate, so I request to stay behind, but Bumbles will hear none of it.

"The rule is every student must get back to the school compound. Only then will you be allowed to disperse," he announces in a curt tone.

Dusk is setting in when the bus driver fires the engine and we edge out of St. Josephs. The bus slowly claws its way uphill toward Hill School.

It is already dark when I get back to the estate.

CHAPTER SIXTEEN

✳ ✳ ✳

YESTERDAY WAS THE second time St. Josephs has licked Hill School in a debating competition, and Bumbles is as sore as a boil, ready to be lanced.

We are in history class, our textbooks out, ready to discuss how the Zulu and Nguni wars caused the Mfecane crushing, but Bumbles has no intention of discussing African history. Not just yet.

"Allegiance and loyalty are two important traits in life," Bumbles stares at the ceiling, sticks out two fingers, and says, "You cannot serve two masters." He steals a glance my way and then shifts his eyes back to the ceiling.

Where is this going? I think. Clearly, yesterday's events aren't over and forgotten.

"It's fine to feel attached to old friends and places you have left behind, but one must make a choice whether to move on into the future or to continue hanging on to the past. And trust me, the latter is a bad choice," Bumbles rambles on, and it's obvious the man has not put the debate debacle behind him.

It is true that when the scores were announced I had clapped, which was the right thing to do. After all, we'd been taught lots of times to be good losers and to cheer our opponents when they turned out to be the better ones. And yesterday we were outmatched. It was only Lillian's individual brilliance that saved us from total embarrassment.

"It seems we have a Trojan horse here in Hill School," Bumbles concludes and then moves on to our history lesson.

For the rest of the day, my mind is on this "Trojan horse." I try to figure out what a horse could possibly have to do with yesterday's debate.

AT HOME IN the evening I'm still puzzling over it.

"Deno, what's a Trojan horse?" I ask.

"How am I supposed to know?"

BABA COMES HOME LATE, so I'm unable to pick his brain over the mysterious horse until the next evening.

"Baba, is there such a thing as a Trojan horse?"

"It's a fable about a town called Troy, whose secure walls had never been breached until a huge wooden horse was given to them as a present." Baba's face lights up as he explains. "At night, enemy soldiers who had been hiding in the horse emerged and attacked the town and destroyed it."

So, according to Bumbles, I was the St. Josephs' Trojan horse, planted in Hill School to destroy it.

Does that even make sense?

BUMBLE'S DISLIKE FOR ME has heightened. He now looks for all manner of excuses to put me down.

It's Wednesday afternoon, time for prep, when everyone should be minding their own business. But I have become Bumbles's sole business since we visited St. Josephs.

He clears his throat. "I'm sure you all know the story of Androcles and the lion?" He looks my way, and there are smiles all around like everyone except me knows what he is talking about.

Me, I don't smile. I just stare ahead.

"Lumumba here will tell us the story of Androcles," Bumbles says and eyes me from above the rim of his glasses.

Now the whole class is waiting for me to make a fool of myself, which is exactly what Bumbles intends for me to do. How could someone like me know about stuff like that?

But what they don't know is I know the story. Actually, I learned it at my not-so-stupid old school. So I rise from my seat and clear my throat like important people do before speaking. Then I tell them about this crazy guy who pulled a thorn out of a lion's paw, after which the two became friends and the lion wouldn't eat him when it was supposed to.

Kazungu gives me a pitiful look and waits for Bumbles to put me in my place.

When Bumbles skips to another topic, everyone realizes I'm right. Rush gives me a thumbs-up from where he is sitting by the window, while Kazungu spends the rest of the lesson glaring my way.

CHAPTER SEVENTEEN

* * *

"***CHONGOLO MAPIPA! CHONGOLO MAPIPA!***" kids in the estate shout at the top of their voices. It's a Thursday, the last day of the midterm break. It isn't even midmorning, yet the sun is already making its intentions clear.

The garbage collectors are around. I smell the thick stench even before I see their huge green truck inch in from the main road. Two men in green overalls follow behind. They snatch metal garbage bins lined outside the houses. They hoist them over their shoulders and empty the contents into their moving truck.

One of the men is squat with drooping bulldog jowls. The other is lanky and has a ready smile. Unlike his mate who tosses bins high in the air and makes rude gestures, the squat guy is gentle. He empties his bins and places them down like they were made of glass and might break. I follow and watch from a distance.

Bulldog Jowls glances over his shoulder, like he needs to confirm I'm still there. The truck is about to nose back onto the tarmac when he rushes to the front, jerks the cabin door open, hops in, and emerges with a black-and-white football.

"What's your name?" He gestures me forward.

"Lumush."

"That's short for Lumumba?"

Everyone knows that, I say to myself in my mind.

He rubs his palm against the top of my head like Baba often does. I allow him to because I want the football he is carrying. He presses it into my hands and smiles for the first time. His smile is gentle though sad. Maybe it's his face that makes everything about him sad.

"I had a son just about your age. You remind me of him." He turns, waves, and is gone.

I stand there wondering what could have happened to the man's son. Maybe he ran away from home or even died. Could be the reason the man looks so sad.

I toss the ball up and down. It's as good as new. They probably picked it out of the management people's garbage. I'd never throw out such a new ball. Not even now that Baba is a manager.

I'm bouncing my ball up and down when my sixth sense tells me that someone is watching. That's the sense animals rely on that warns them of things they can't see, hear, touch, smell, or taste.

I look over my shoulder and, sure enough, Zgwembe is there. His red eyes are fixed on my ball. He leans against the Zephyr, tossing stuff into the gutter and pretending to mind his own business, when me, I know it's my ball that is his immediate business. He lives with his father, Rasta, in a dirty kiosk under a cluster of flame trees at the north end of the estate.

I try to act as normal as possible, but my heart is beating like a drum. I continue to bounce my ball, but my focus is on Zgwembe. He digs a finger deep into his nose, twirls it. Two big, dirty toes stick out from his canvas shoes. He scratches his head then lifts an arm to scratch under his armpits. He shoves his hand into his shorts to scratch in there too.

I sense Zgwembe is about to make his move. My heart is now hammering so loud Zgwembe surely hears it.

I'm about to bolt off when Dado, Odush, and Mose arrive, standing by my side.

Zgwembe kicks out at the dusty ground to register his frustration and saunters off.

The drumming in my chest subsides.

"Nice ball you have there!" Dado says.

"I got it from the garbage collectors," I say. I don't often lie to Dado. The guy can always tell when you are lying.

"Those management people are crazy. Why would you throw away something that's almost new? Some people have all the luck in the world, yet they throw it away," Dado says and then goes silent.

"Not all management people are like that," I say.

"Oh! I forgot your father is now a manager."

I shrug. "Still, I'd never throw away something as new as this."

"So, when are you people moving to those huge houses up the hill? Maybe you should start by moving into the ghost house. Then in a couple of days you would all be ghosts—*awoooooooooooo*," Odush slaps his palm on his mouth.

"There is no way I'm moving out of the estate. It's hard enough being in that lousy school," I say, as if I have a choice. I've been praying Baba does not get a house up the hill.

"Cool ball, yah?" Mose turns to Odush and bounces my ball up and down.

Odush stands to one side like he doesn't want to be part of the game. It's what the cut has done to him. It's made him think he is all grown up, yet he still wants to hang out with us.

Dado's eyes are fixed on my ball like he sees something we don't. "One day I will join Railways and be a manager," he says. He peers into the sky as though there is proof of what he'll be written in the clouds.

"See who wants to be a manager!" Odush rolls his eyes.

"I'll be that and maybe more. I could even be a super-manager," Dado says, making us all gaze about in wonder.

"And what do super-managers do? Where do they live?"

"They issue orders to the other managers and live at the highest point on the hill," Dado says.

"Must be somewhere in heaven," Odush says.

"Dado is right. I've heard my father say that Railways has a top manager called the managing director. All other managers work under him," I say.

"You are always siding with Dado even when you know he is lying," Odush eyes me from under bunched brows. "Now you are trying to cheat us that there is one super-manager, who controls all the other managers."

"Once I'm a super-manager, I'll lock up all the managers who steal coffee from the bogies and also those who steal medicine from the dispensaries. My mum says there are no medicines in the dispensary because the managers keep stealing them," Dado continues.

"And what makes you think they'll let you do that?" Mose says. "They'll gang up against you and throw you out."

"Not all the managers steal," I say.

"Now that your father is a manager, he will soon be like the rest of them," Odush waves his hand dismissively.

I remember Baba's story about people who a few years back had nothing but tattered pants and broken shoes, but now have tons of money to burn. Baba says that some of them have so much, if it were all laid out in ten-shilling notes on the ground, it would stretch all the way from Mombasa to Kisumu and back. I don't even think there is that much money in the whole world. Not even the management people from up the hill, with their gated compounds, cars, and garages, can have that kind of money, even if they stole. But maybe it's just a story. Baba keeps changing it, so that sometimes the money the thieves have is enough to boil ten huge metal barrels of water, if it were stacked up and lit into a bonfire. Other times it's enough to cover the entire grass on ten football pitches. I once asked him where they stashed it all, and he said they had carted it abroad. Is it even possible to carry so much money out of the country? I think Baba just makes up these stories.

"Who cares if people steal coffee from the bogies or medicine from the dispensaries? They can go ahead and close all the dispensaries, for all I care," Odush snaps me back to the present. "All they do in those dispensaries is stick needles into people's backsides."

"Where would you go if you had malaria and the dispensaries were closed?" Mose asks.

"He would probably call those Riswa guys in white robes," Dado laughs. "My mum says they are just con men looking for money. How do you expect to get healed by some crazy guy beating a drum and screaming at the top of his voice?"

"When my sister Anjie was sick she didn't need any dispensary," Odush says. "Those Riswa people just beat their drums until she was well."

"You should have had your Riswa people beat drums and dance for Lumush when he broke his arm. Then, *Sim sala bim*, his arm would be healed," Dado says and, except for Odush, we all laugh.

CHAPTER EIGHTEEN

✳ ✳ ✳

"**HEY! COME SEE THIS,**" Odush shouts out but we ignore him.

We are already at our favorite spot behind the estate. I'm juggling my ball. I tap it up with my foot, keeping it in the air while counting. I'm at forty-seven; three taps away from the fifty Mose managed.

"You people better come and see this," Odush persists. He has a black-and-white photograph in his right hand and a brown diary in his left. The photo has two white men standing next to a smiling white woman with a baby in her arms. The baby has long straight hair and looks like the dolls Mama buys Awino. Behind them is a Bedford lorry.

"That lorry looks like the one in Mwachuma's yard," Mose says and reaches for the photo, but Odush steps away and shoves it into his pocket before Mose can grab it.

Me, my mind is racing. The second man in the picture has a striking resemblance to my teacher, Bumbles.

"Where did you find the picture?" I ask.

"In between the springs of the Zephyr's torn back seat."

"Are sure you found it in the car?" Mose wants to know.

"No, I pulled it out from a magic hat," Odush sneers and allows us to peer at the photo again.

The words "*Cynthia, Anna, my bro, Eric, and I, with the new lorry,*" are scrawled on the back in red.

"Can I take a closer look at the second man in the picture?" My hand reaches out, but Odush snatches the picture away from me.

"Just because there is a Bedford lorry in the photo doesn't mean it is the same one that's in Mwachuma's yard," Dado argues, but my eyes are glued to the shorter of the two men in the picture. The pinched lips, the mustache, the ears pressed back against the sides of his head, the angle he has tilted his head away, convince me it is Bumbles.

"The one to the left in the photo is my class teacher, Bumbles," I blurt out, and then we are all scrambling for the picture again and the more we pore over it the more I'm convinced it's Bumbles.

"How sure are you?" Dado manages to snatch the photo from Odush.

"That's Bumbles alright, no doubt about it. I'm in his class every single day and can't mistake him."

"If it's your teacher in the photo, then he has to be 'Eric,' " Dado hands me the photo.

I again stare at it, I turn it around to study the words written in red. "What if it was Bumbles who wrote on the back? Then it would mean Eric is Mr. Swiney and Bumbles is his brother," I say.

"You should find out from your father if Swiney's name was

Eric. If not, then it's Bumbles who is Eric." Dado hands me the picture and I focus on the lorry.

"Only the letter 'K' and the number '2' are visible on the registration plate of the lorry in the picture," I say.

"Can anyone remember the numbers on Mwachuma's lorry?" Dado asks.

"There certainly is a 'K,'" Odush beams.

"All cars in the country have the letter 'K' on the plate number. It stands for Kenya," Dado says, and Odush is no longer beaming. "We'd have to get past Mwachuma's mongrel if we're to confirm if it is the same lorry. And even if it is, it could be that Swiney sold it to Mwachuma before he died."

"Could we also take a look at the diary?" I reach out for the brown diary Odush is still holding, and suddenly all attention is on it.

When Odush spreads it on the hood of the Zephyr, the first thing we notice is that the name Eric Swiney appears on the first page. We then pore over the entries scrawled in the writer's slanting hand:

4th May

A tall man came to my office and threatened me. He wanted a consignment of coffee the police had detained together with a lorry released. He said the police had informed him they would only release them if I authorized it. Told him it was stolen property and only a court order would cause its release.

8th May

Cynthia informed me there were strangers outside our gate at dusk when I was away. They never knocked nor asked to be allowed in. Half an hour later someone tossed a rock and shattered our living room window. Cynthia was scared as hell.

9th May

Reported the incident at the railway police station. The officers laughed and said I was being paranoid and that it was most probably a bunch of naughty kids who broke the window.

16th May

The tall man paid me another visit. This time he came with a man who had a black eye patch. The one-eyed man coughed most of the time and did not say a word. He left all the talking to the tall one. I told him nothing had changed and my stance was still the same. I later discovered that the man with the black eye patch owns a metal scrapyard. Seemed like a shifty character.

2nd June

This morning I found a note slipped under my office door, with the words YOU HAVE A LOVELY FAMILY. PITY IF SOMETHING HAPPENED TO THEM.

Very scary, but not budging. This coffee theft must stop.

Odush's jaw is hanging loose. Mose's eyes are so wide open his eyeballs could fall out of their sockets. I'm not certain how I look.

"Wow!" I turn to Dado, who shakes his head as though from a dream.

"We should turn this over to the police," Odush pulls the diary away.

"I think we should try and get to the bottom of this," Dado looks my way for support.

I nod, though I'm not sure why.

"You people are crazy," Odush taps his forefinger to his head. "If the man did not commit suicide, as it seems from his diary, then he was killed. We would also be in danger."

"Let's turn the diary over to the police, get it out of our hands," Odush says.

"If the suicide man . . . no, let's call him Mr. Swiney. If Mr. Swiney reported to the police about his smashed window and they laughed it off as the actions of some naughty kids, what makes you think they will take us seriously?" Dado asks. "What is in the diary is not proof of any wrongdoing."

"But they threatened his family in the note he found under his office door," Odush says.

"He doesn't say he knew who wrote it," Dado argues.

"So what do we do with this stuff?" Odush pulls the diary from his pocket.

"Just as I said, we keep it until we are sure of what happened," Dado says.

"I'm not going home with these things," Odush hands the diary and photo to Dado. "You keep them."

"Why don't we hide them exactly where you found them," Dado suggests, and it seems like a good idea, so that's what we do.

CHAPTER NINETEEN

*** * ***

ODUSH HAS HIS EYES and mouth wide open. Mose tugs at my shirt and points at a distant figure, rolling toward us like a locomotive.

It's Apima, the woman who owns the local drinking den. She has one hand pressed to her side to keep her lesso wrap in place. Could be it is also to guard the money she ties under it. She reaches the Zephyr, slaps her hands against its sides to stop, and I swear, it moves a few inches.

Apima slumps to the ground behind the Zephyr. Her breathing is labored, like she's played a full football match. She presses a fat forefinger to her lips to warn us to stay silent. Her massive shoulders rise and fall with her breathing.

Two policemen in uniform appear from the front of the estate. Their eyes dart about like they are looking for someone. They cup their hands against their foreheads to shield their eyes from the sun.

Apima stays hidden.

THE PEOPLE OF RAILWAY ESTATE have learned to live with Apima and her brew. Lots of men and even some women spend their evenings drinking the illicit changaa she brews in Block 12. Mama says they are all weak-of-spirit and in need of prayers.

The talk is that Apima dips charms in her brew to keep people coming back for more. Me, I wonder what kind of charms can make grown men and women keep going back to Apima's house to drink changaa.

Even Odush, who pretends to be an expert over grown-up matters, is unable to properly explain:

"People use charms to control others. They don't last forever, and just like batteries, charms also become useless after a while," he says.

THERE WERE ALSO those who considered Apima an angel. They could never forget how she took in Makaratasi's baby when nobody wanted the newborn child.

It all started when the eagle-eyed women of Railway Estate noticed the bulge under the madwoman's dirty dress. At first they dismissed it as a result of what she had eaten, but with every passing day Makaratasi's belly grew bigger and bigger. Not that it stopped her from collecting discarded paper, stuffing it into her sack, and depositing it behind Mwachuma's scrapyard, where she slept. Soon it became obvious there was a baby in that swelling belly.

As the months went by, Makaratasi's belly continued to grow until it seemed it would burst open. Then one rainy morning, loud screams were heard from near the scrapyard and Dado's mum was the first to get there. In no time she appeared with a new baby wrapped in a towel, and the whole estate was ecstatic. But no one wanted to take the baby home, so Apima offered to take her. Four years on, Makaratasi's little girl, Tabasamu, still lived with Apima, who treated her like her own.

LONG AFTER THE policemen have left, Apima attempts to rise from where she is seated behind the Zephyr, but collapses right back onto the ground.

Dado steps forward and offers her a hand. He tries to help her up but she is too heavy. It is only after we all intervene that she manages to rise to her feet. She gives Dado a quick peck on the cheek and she is off.

We watch her massive body shaking like jelly inside her dress as she goes.

IT IS NOT LIKE THE police don't know what goes on inside Block 12. Once a week they raid the place and march Apima away. A couple of hours later she is back, selling her brew. Everyone says she gives them something small. Then they are all smiles, and have lots of good things to say about her.

"Has anyone seen me in their house looking for customers? I sit right here and all those men bring themselves to Block 12. Their wives ought to ask why their men spend time here rather than in their homes," Apima challenges anyone who accuses her of spoiling the men of Railway Estate.

However, things changed a bit when a man called Stingo died less than four months after he moved into the estate.

Stingo lived in Block 24, close to the social hall. He always wore a white fedora with a thin yellow band around the side and never took it off. People said he worked from one of the many offices in the brown building that housed the railway headquarters. No one knew exactly what he did, and so rumors about him swelled.

Showing up a few weeks after the mysterious death of the white family on Desai Street, people said he was a police officer, working undercover, and maybe he was.

Stingo would stop over by the old Zephyr and walk around it, shaking his head and marveling at the old car. He once referred to the person who abandoned it as a fool. He then asked if we knew who the owner was, and I almost blurted out that it belonged to Swiney, before Dado elbowed me. Maybe the man was investigating the whole affair and I would end up as a suspect, Dado warned.

Odush swore he once saw Stingo come from the direction of the ghost house, before the man disappeared. But then anyone going to the railway headquarters, where Stingo's offices were situated, had to go past the ghost house, and perhaps Stingo was just going to work. You had to take Odush's word with a whole tablespoon of salt.

Most evenings Stingo would stop over at Apima's in Block 12 for a quick drink. He kept to himself and spoke little. Someone said they had seen a gun under his shirt, so he had to be a security agent.

And so the mystery of who Stingo was remained unsolved. After a while, people accepted him as a resident of Railway Estate.

He interfered with no one and seemed to mind his own business. Even when one of Apima's regulars accosted him and accused him of being an agent of the state sent to spy on people, Stingo simply downed his drink and walked away. Then Stingo disappeared. When for three straight days no one saw him emerge from his house and his door remained locked from the inside, they alerted Tumbo, the estate overseer, who forced the lock. They found Stingo's lifeless body on a chair in his living room, with a charcoal jiko stove by his side. Those who were present said he had a nasty black bruise on the head.

I remember Baba saying it could be foul play. Who would be stupid enough to lock themselves in a room with a burning jiko and the deadly carbon monoxide it releases? Besides, the man had a bruise on his head.

TWO WEEKS AFTER STINGO'S DEATH, a woman in a tight skirt and red lipstick had appeared with a teenage boy who resembled the dead man. Two men helped them load Stingo's furniture onto the back of a pickup truck, under Tumbo's supervision. They then drove off and it was as if Stingo had never existed.

CHAPTER TWENTY

✳ ✳ ✳

THE WORDS "WE BUI SCRAP METAL" are written in bold letters at the entrance of Mwachuma's scrapyard. Yet the man lives alone in his littered yard. Could be he considers his mongrel, Tarzan, leashed in a corner, as his business partner.

Mwachuma buys all the scrap metal he can lay his hands on. He calls it dead metal and says he is there to give it a decent burial. When he is in a good mood he will adjust his black eye patch and demonstrate the fighting skills he learned during the Mau Mau War, when he lost his eye.

His left hand extended, the right one on his chest, his head tilted, he will pretend he is holding a gun, take aim, shout—"boom." He will repeat the maneuver over and over until he is out of breath, wheezing and coughing.

He never seems to leave his yard, yet he knows everything that goes on in the estate. Perched on a metal bin, his knees drawn up and his shoulders hunched, Mwachuma's tiny, bald head sticks out from his neck, making him resemble a vulture.

Mwachuma pretends he hasn't seen us walk into his yard. He

lifts his nose to sniff the air, then blocks one nostril, blows hard through the other, and wipes his snort-smeared hand against his dirty trousers. He reaches for a half-smoked cigarette from the back of his ear and lights up. Smoke exits from his mouth and nose, before he erupts into loud coughing, like there is a battle raging in his sunken chest.

Tarzan stirs from behind the old Bedford lorry in a corner of the yard. I've seen the film *Tarzan*, where this white guy with golden hair and a strip of skin for a skirt is lost in the jungle. He speaks animal language and sometimes rides an elephant. He swings from tree to tree. Only, he is white with blond hair and not black like Mwachuma's dog.

Mwachuma is in no hurry. He slides off his perch, places a foot on the ground. He sucks at his cigarette one last time, tossing it onto the dusty ground. He coughs to clear his throat, then spits. With every step, he winces and bites his lower lip like he is stepping on shards of glass. It takes him forever to reach us.

"I told you the guy has jiggers," Odush whispers. "I've seen people in our shaggs walk that way. After the fleas' eggs were dug out from their skin, they walked normally again."

"What is it you kids want?" He scratches his big belly and we cover our mouths to keep from laughing. "I don't have time to stand around doing nothing," he says, as if he ever does anything other than smoke and scratch.

"We want to buy your scrapyard," Odush says, and we all laugh.

"I don't have time to waste. Tell me what you want."

Dado pulls out the brass rod we've decided to use as an excuse to enter Mwachuma's yard. He hands it to Mwachuma, who pulls out his Okapi knife and scrapes it.

"I'll give you two shillings for it," Mwachuma says and tosses it into his heap.

"We won't accept anything less than three shillings," Dado replies.

But all our eyes are trained on the green Bedford lorry.

Its front number plate is missing. Could be the rear one is still there. But who is going to find out with that black mongrel leashed beside it?

"You're the smart one, aren't you?" Mwachuma pulls out three shillings and hands the money to Dado. "You should be a businessman."

"The old Bedford lorry, it's been in your yard for years. What do you intend to do with it?" I edge in that general direction, but my eyes are on Tarzan, who hasn't moved a muscle.

"It still can't move, but once it is repaired it will transport lots of goods," Mwachuma boasts. "When the railway grinds to a halt, as it certainly must, road transport will be the way to go."

"And what makes you think anyone would want to carry anything in that old thing? What does the number plate read, anyway? K . . . what?" Dado asks.

Mwachuma does not respond.

"No one has ever seen your lorry move," Odush cuts in, and Mwachuma's eyes dart to the ground near the lorry's tires.

"How do you know that the railway will grind to a halt?" I ask to draw Mwachuma's attention away from the lorry.

Mwachuma ignores my question at first. "Those tire marks you see were made when some mechanics towed the lorry a short distance while making repairs on it. And as for the railway grinding to a halt, how do I know that night follows day? Of course it does. Everybody knows the railway will not last long. Not with all the stealing going on."

"I know you're eyeing the railway, hoping it fails so you can get scrap metal," I say.

"I certainly wouldn't mind so much scrap."

"Is that why you have Nairobi city council manhole covers here in your yard? The one outside our house disappeared and now there's a gaping hole," Odush says.

What's wrong with the guy? Next thing he will be telling Mwachuma about the diary we found.

"I think you kids should leave, now," Mwachuma bristles.

"Not until we see the number plate of your lorry," Odush says, and I could kill him.

"Whose property has Mwachuma stolen? The stuff here doesn't belong to anyone. It's all brought in by people in need of money. Who has seen me leave this yard to look for scrap? People bring it to me, like you did that brass rod. Now get out of here before I throw you out."

We don't move until he reaches into his pocket and we remember the wicked-looking Okapi knife he used to scrape our brass rod, then we run out to the entrance, where we sing:

"Old Mwachuma has a jigger in his toe
Old Mwachuma has a jigger in his toe

Old Mwachuma has a jigger in his toe
And that's the reason he can't walk straight."

Mwachuma makes to hobble in our direction, changes his mind, turns to where Tarzan is leashed, and bends to let loose the growling dog. But we are long gone.

"WE OUGHT TO TELL Tumbo about the manhole covers in Mwachuma's yard," Odush says.

"And who says he doesn't know? Apondi says Tumbo is the biggest crook around. She's good at digging out such things," I say. "Mwachuma's got to be involved with something more sinister than scrap metal."

"Come on, let's go buy mangoes with the money we got from Mwachuma," Dado interrupts, and we troop toward the entrance of St. Josephs.

Mama Maembe has a big wooden crucifix dangling from her neck and sits on a low stool, a metal basin full of mangoes at her feet. She peels the top off each mango with a sharp flick of her knife, then slices the sides so they hang outward in flaps. She sprinkles ground red pepper mixed with salt on them. We sink our teeth into the mangoes, sucking in air to cool the burning sensation of the ground pepper.

"We could sneak into Mwachuma's yard at night to see the lorry's license plate. I think the thing can move," Dado mumbles and reaches into his mouth with his thumb and forefinger to pull out mango fibers lodged between his teeth.

"Aaa! Me, I'm not going anywhere near that madman. You saw

the knife he had and that dog. Worse still, the man could have a gun. You've seen the shooting moves he makes." I shake my head.

"I'm not scared of the man, he can barely walk," Odush says.

"You're always talking tough, but at the first sign of trouble you're off like a jet plane," Dado challenges him.

"We could do it at night," he ignores Dado.

"Not with that black mongrel in the yard. The thing could be sick. You've seen the stuff that comes out of its mouth. When you get bitten by a sick dog, you start barking like it and biting people. Then they start howling, too," Mose curls his lips.

"Do you know how many injections they give you when you are bitten by a sick dog? Seventeen injections, and all in the stomach," Dado says.

"You mean, all at once?" I stare at Dado.

"Oh yes!"

"That's a lie. Nobody ever gets injected seventeen times," Odush says.

"You go and get yourself bitten by Mwachuma's mongrel and see if the drumming and singing of those Riswa people can save you," he tells Odush.

"There's no way I'm going near that mongrel," Odush says.

"Neither am I," Mose says.

Now that we have decided we aren't going back to the scrapyard, we head for the old Zephyr. It's where we always end up.

CHAPTER TWENTY-ONE

✱ ✱ ✱

MOSE, ODUSH, AND I are behind the estate blocks, strolling toward the Zephyr, when a man in a yellow T-shirt leaps over the iron fence that separates the railway yard from the estate and lands a few feet from where we are. We are about to take to our heels but then realize the man means us no harm, so we pause.

The man must have hurt his leg because he limps off in the direction of the rail overpass. He glances over his shoulder as he goes.

"Did you see that? He had bloodstains on his shirt," Mose says.

"Why would he jump over the fence?" I say, and just then the sound of a siren reaches our ears.

A blue police car shoots in from the main road and screeches to a halt. Two police officers leap out of the car just as a second man tries to scramble over the metal fence. He reaches for something under his jacket, but too late, the police officers grab him from under his shoulders and pin him to the ground. The man tries to kick at them until one of the officers pulls out a gun, then he stops struggling. They handcuff his wrists and sit him on the ground.

"Hey! You kids shouldn't be here," one of the officers shouts, and we race off to the front of the estate.

"That policeman pulled out a gun like in those cowboy films," Mose says when we reach my house.

"How do you know it was a gun?" Odush asks.

"Who doesn't know what a gun looks like?" Mose says.

"If it wasn't a gun then what was it? It had to be a gun, that black thing," I say. "Policemen carry guns and they are allowed to use them."

"Do you think he would have shot the man if he tried to run?" Mose asks.

"No, I don't think so. They would just have overpowered him. Those officers are strong. And you also don't shoot people unless your life is in danger," I say.

"Everyone seems to be heading back there, let's go see what's happening," Mose says, and we head back to where the police are.

The man is still seated on the ground with his wrists hand-cuffed. Three more uniformed policemen have joined the earlier two. They are combing the grass around the arrested man, searching for something.

"Maybe the man dropped a key or some secret code on a piece of paper," Odush says.

"Or even the money he stole," Mose says.

"How do you know he stole money?" I ask.

BY NOON the policemen are still combing the scene. One of them takes photographs, while another in a white lab coat concentrates on the metal fence.

"The man in the coat is probably looking for fingerprints," Dado says when he arrives. "I read somewhere that when you touch something you leave your fingerprints on it."

"Just like when you touch a glass surface," I say.

"Did you also know that in the whole world, there are no two people who have similar fingerprints?" Dado asks, and Odush gives him a look that says, *go cheat someone else.*

"That's true," I say. "Once the police get the fingerprints of the man who got away, they will be able to trace him."

"And how is that even possible?" Odush wants to know.

"I think the police have everyone's fingerprints and name stored somewhere. So all they need to do is compare them," Dado says, and I'm wondering if that is even possible.

THE SUN IS almost setting when the police finally drive off with the arrested man. By then practically everybody has left. *If that is what they do most of the time, then police work must be really boring,* I think to myself.

BABA BRINGS UP the arrest after we've had supper. He says the man was part of a gang that had already offloaded lots of bags of coffee from a bogie before the police were alerted. The coffee was destined for Mombasa but had been diverted to a deserted part of the railway yard.

"Once I discovered about the diversion, I alerted the police," Baba says. "Some of the men escaped in a lorry with some coffee."

"I'm sure the police will arrest all the others," I say. "I saw them get their fingerprints from the metal fence after they jumped over it."

"So now you have become a policeman? Could you help get those plates to the kitchen instead of talking about things that don't concern you?" Mama snaps at me and I'm off, but I notice Baba smiling.

THE FOLLOWING DAY there is a story about the coffee theft in Baba's newspaper. Baba reads it aloud. His tone rises and his eyes brighten when he reaches the section that mentions his name:

"Mr. Onimbo, a railway employee, saved the day by alerting the police. Were it not for this honest employee's quick action the corporation would have suffered significant loss, the Managing Director was quoted as saying."

I wait until Baba leaves the room before I tear off the page and shove it into my pocket so that I can show it to Mose and the others.

CHAPTER TWENTY-TWO

* * *

THE APRIL HOLIDAYS are upon us. The rain hammers against our iron roofs before rushing to the ground to form puddles. Still, we hang out at the back of the estate near the Zephyr, not worried about getting wet.

But Apondi soon shows up to ruin the fun. "Your mother says she is coming out to whip your backside if you don't get out of the rain. Who do you think will take you to the hospital when you get malaria?"

Malaria comes from mosquito bites and not from the rain. But who wants to argue when there is the threat of Mama's switch? So I slink indoors to find other things to do. You would think the rain has colluded with Mama because it doesn't let up until dusk.

IT'S THE SAFARI RALLY SEASON. My favorite driver is a Kenyan man nicknamed the Flying Sikh. He always wears a turban and a smile.

Mose supports the Datsun team and Dado the Peugeot. Dado loves Peugeots.

Odush has no preference. He says the Safari Rally is kiddish. The stupid cut has filled his head with all manner of grown-up stuff, but it hasn't given him new friends, so he still has to hang out with us.

"Why are you here, talking about the rally if it's kids' stuff? Why don't you go find some place where you can do adult stuff?" I ask as we're sitting around the Zephyr.

"Does this look like your living room?" Odush scowls.

IT IS THE LAST LEG of the rally. The leading cars are expected in Nairobi the day after tomorrow. Baba's radio says the competing cars are in a place called Turkana, with a white guy in the lead. One of the Asians that Amin expelled from Uganda is hot on the white guy's tail. The man is now a Kenyan citizen, and he's the country's best hope.

It begins to rain again. The rain's patter against the iron roof drowns Baba's radio. His attempts at increasing the volume do not help. The announcer's voice is replaced by static. Baba switches off the radio.

SAVE FOR A light drizzle that petered out in the morning, the sky is clear and it promises to be a bright day. We are out by the old Zephyr.

"I think the Kenyan-Asian will win," I say.

"The man is not even Kenyan," Odush snaps. "Just because Amin sent him here doesn't make him Kenyan."

"So what makes one a Kenyan?"

"You need to be born here."

"Deno was born in Jinja when our father was still working in Uganda. So you want to say he is not Kenyan?"

"That's different."

"How is it different?"

"You just shut your mouth," Odush says, and I mimic him, because that's what he always says when he loses an argument.

"Lumush, your mum's calling you," Apondi shouts out from the corner of the block.

"Coming," I shout back, but I'm not really. Mama just wants to know where we are and what we are up to. It's the reason she sends Apondi to spy on us.

Apondi doesn't wait to see whether I'm following her. She adjusts her headscarf and disappears the way she came. I know she will tell Mama that we are behind the block, playing pata potea and causing trouble. She never tells Mama the truth.

Tapa tapa tapa tapa—I hear the sound of pati patis and I know it is Njish even before I turn around. She has a flower-patterned dress and a kiondo bag strapped over her shoulder. Her blue pati patis slap against the soles of her feet. She glowers at Odush, then turns and smiles at me as she hurries past.

Odush continues teasing me long after Njish is gone.

"I can still hear your heart beating from here," Odush says and shoves his hand under his shirt to mimic a heartbeat.

"Shut up."

We are still kidding around when I spot Njish hurrying back. Odush steps forward to block her path. When she steps away from him, he swings right back into her path and again she side-steps him.

Amused at his silly game, Njish plays along until he makes to grab her basket and that is when she slaps him hard on the cheek.

Odush stands there stunned. For a while he doesn't move, as though he's turned into a statue. When he explodes into action and goes for her, I lunge at him and knock him to the ground.

After that everything is fuzzy. I remember Odush rising in slow motion, a furious look on his face, and I hear Mose go, "Oh! Oh!" and I'm lashing out again and Odush is on the ground a second time and I have this urgent desire to flee.

Then Dado is between us and my vision clears.

Odush rises and walks away with his head lowered.

"IT'S TOO EARLY TO TELL who will win," Odush mumbles. He hasn't said much since yesterday's incident. Still, I know he isn't one to carry a grudge. I would love to tell him I'm sorry but I don't know how to start. His lower lip is still red and swollen.

"You better move away from the road, so those rally cars don't run you over," I reach out and pull him back just to show there are no hard feelings.

His face lights up into a smile.

We hear a distant purr that builds up until it is a roar, before a spotlight beam flashes out through the heavy rain. A car leaps forward, its colored nose raised, as though it wants to fly up into the air. Its wheels screech against the asphalt as it does a side spin before straightening out, and then it is gone.

I only realize I am hugging Dado when he pushes me away.

Mose is screaming at the top of his voice, like the winning driver is his blood brother.

A few minutes later the second car, driven by a white guy, tears past and we clap and cheer until Dado reminds us that the guy is gunning to beat our man, and then we are jeering even though the car is long gone.

We are still waiting for the other rally cars when a white pickup truck shoots out from behind the roundabout. It slams into a lamppost, flips over, and rolls several times before landing in a ditch. We rush forward to help free the driver from the car's cabin.

"Get away from the road," a policeman shouts. "This rally makes people lose their heads. If you aren't careful, another driver will run the lot of you over."

Reluctantly, we move away.

"Did you notice his shoe had come off? It always happens in a car accident," Odush says as we watch from a distance.

The accident victim is seated on the grass and is bleeding from a gash on his forehead. He stares out into space as he waits for an ambulance. He has only one shoe on.

Back at the estate people are celebrating. They hop up and down and hug like they will share the top rally prize. I wonder how Amin now feels, after the man he expelled from Uganda has won the Safari Rally for Kenya.

CHAPTER TWENTY-THREE

✳ ✳ ✳

"YOU WOULD DIE FOR ME, Lumush, wouldn't you?" Njish wants to know. She has her hands clasped behind her back, her eyes glued to a spot above my head, like there is another me floating there.

I'm next to Mama Nandwa's kiosk, a packet of sugar in my right hand. I shift my weight from one foot to the other, trying to figure out what it is all about this time.

"You heard what I said, Lumumba," Njish now addresses me by my full name like most grown-ups do. "Would you die for me?"

"Mmmm!" I say, though I don't know what this dying business is all about. Bumbles wants me to die for our flag and country. Njish now needs me to die for her. Baba often says a true man must find something they are ready and willing to die for, but how many things can one man die for? How many times can someone even die?

Njish is waiting for an answer, so I nod. You know, when Njish looks at you with those big brown eyes, you can do nothing but agree with everything she says.

"Thanks for protecting me from that monster, Odush," Njish says, and I realize that's the reason for this talk about dying.

Hell! Does she have any idea how scared I was when I punched Odush? I could have lost an arm or a leg. Then I would be limping all over the place. Maybe I could have even died for real.

"Will you do something else for me, Lumush?"

"Yes," I say, and I'm scared she is about to ask me to do something even worse than dying.

"Will you kiss me?" She leans so close I can feel her warm breath on my face.

I look around to see if there is anyone watching.

"You are afraid someone will see you kissing me?"

"No! It is because I have never done it before."

"How will I know you care if you don't kiss me? Now you go on and kiss me, Lumush," she says and her dimpled cheek is right on my lips.

I kiss her quickly.

"You see, it is not that bad," she laughs.

Long after she is gone I can still feel her soft cheek on my lips and the sweet scent of Patco sweets.

CHAPTER TWENTY-FOUR

* * *

APONDI TELLS MAMA THAT I visited the ghost house on Desai Street at night. She has been threatening to do so, but for one reason or the other, she hasn't until today. But last night I told her she sounded like a crow when she sang. That must have really hurt her, because she takes her singing seriously and believes she has a wonderful voice.

"It's a lie," I protest to Mama.

But Mama believes Apondi, so she sends for a switch from the mapera tree behind our house. She makes me lie flat on my belly on the living room floor.

Baba tries to intervene. He asks me to assure them it will never happen again, but Mama is beyond listening.

"Someone has to do this, or one day your son will get himself killed," Mama warns. "Lumumba, you know I love you and I'm doing this to make you a better person?" she brings the switch down hard on my bunched buttocks.

I nod in between tears.

"You know I feel pain when I see the tears in your eyes?"

I again nod, but each time the switch whizzes down, the only thing on my mind is how I am going to give Mose a black eye once this is over.

CORPORAL PUNISHMENT has no place in civilized society; at least that is what Bumbles says. That's the reason we carry conduct cards in Hill School. Three demerits on your card and you are in for detention on Saturday. Three consecutive detentions and you are suspended. I guess three consecutive suspensions would have you expelled, but who knows? No one ever has had three consecutive suspensions. Maybe they'd just ask you to empty your locker and leave for good.

The first time I heard the term "corporal punishment" I asked Deno what it meant. He joked that it was when you got punished by a corporal.

I suspected Deno was kidding and so I asked Baba, who told me it was physical punishment, like when someone gets caned. Now I know that what Mama does to us with her switch is corporal punishment, which Bumbles says is primitive.

No one can best Mama in the corporal punishment business. She canes us out of love; at least that is what she says. Even when I'm writhing on her floor and my backside is on fire, she says she is the one in pain.

Me, I can do without her kind of love.

I have three demerits on my conduct card. The first was for lateness and the other two for insubordination. They are all from Bumbles. Three demerits equal detention, so I will be in school for half the day, on Saturday, raking leaves off the quad when I should be playing ball with Dado and the other guys.

Back at St. Josephs, a couple of strokes of the cane would have been sufficient. But this is Hill School, and Hill School does not do corporal punishment.

At St. Josephs, they caned you for everything, even though they never called it corporal punishment. You wrote out wrong answers for the weekly tests, you got caned; you made noise, you got caned; you arrived late, you got whacked right there at the gate. They would even cane you some more for not wincing in pain.

Me, I think they should have just allocated everyone a number of strokes in advance. Then we would save everyone the trouble by presenting ourselves each morning to receive our quota of caning before entering class.

CHAPTER TWENTY-FIVE

✶ ✶ ✶

IT'S MWAKIO, a little bowlegged boy from Block 11, who sees the body first. He pauses, clutching the packet of milk his mother had sent him to buy to his side, sucking in the yellow snot dripping down his nose, before sprinting off as fast as his legs can allow. He can't wait to tell his parents about the green lorry that has crashed into the ditch behind the slaughterhouse and the body of a boy lying in the road.

They dismiss him as a little liar and threaten to spank him for fibbing, but he insists it's the truth. So they accompany him to the spot and find the lifeless body of a boy in a blue T-shirt lying across the road and a green Bedford lorry, its front wheels and cabin in the ditch, its rear wheels suspended in the air.

They check the boy's pulse and confirm he is dead. There are blood smudges on the sides of the cabin door of the lorry.

Not long after, someone identifies the dead boy as Zgwembe.

Amimo the charcoal dealer says he heard tires screeching in the dead of the night, followed by a loud bang, then silence. "You can see from the skid marks that the driver braked hard before crashing into the ditch," he concludes.

"The driver must have run away," someone says.

"Whoever was driving the lorry must have been doing something illegal. Otherwise why not report the accident, if it was one?"

"Someone should hop in to find out what's in the back," Amimo says.

"No! You shouldn't do that before the police arrive," someone warns, and so people just mill around the scene.

"Who will go and find the boy's father?" Apondi says, her voice hoarse with emotion. She unties her lesso wrapper and uses it to cover the body.

"The man is probably in his kiosk, high on the stuff he sells," Amimo lets out a nervous laugh.

"Could it be Mwachuma's lorry?" Dado whispers to me. He was one of the first people to get to the scene.

"It's a Bedford and it's green like his," I say.

"Why don't we slip over to Mwachuma's yard and see if his lorry is still there?" Mose suggests.

"There will be enough time for that. For now let's hang around and see what happens when the police arrive," Dado says.

"Now you see why I suggested we give the photo and diary to the police. By now they would have arrested that thug, Mwachuma," Odush mumbles.

This is something that is really bothering me. What if Mwachuma *is* responsible for Zgwembe's death? What if we had handed over the photo and diary to the police as Odush had suggested? Maybe then they would have arrested Mwachuma, and Zgwembe would still be alive.

HOURS LATER, the police are yet to arrive.

Tumbo elbows through the mass of bodies that still mill around the Bedford lorry. He unbuttons his jacket, wipes the sweat off his face, and addresses those who have gathered around the lorry.

"The police have been notified and will soon be here. They will be able to find out who was driving the lorry and who owns it," Tumbo says.

"Stop pretending you don't know who the lorry belongs to," Odush shouts.

Dado elbows him, but Odush ignores it.

"That lorry belongs to your one-eyed friend," he shouts out.

Tumbo clears his throat to speak but his words are stuck in his throat. His mouth stays open for a while but no words come out. When he manages to speak his tone is threatening.

"You shouldn't make such accusations. You could easily get in trouble. What do you know about anything anyway?"

"Is it Mwachuma's lorry or not?" a voice calls out from the crowd, and it is none other than Apima. "I've heard talk of that old lorry roaring across the estate by night and doing all sorts of shady things. Yet Mwachuma parks it in that junkyard during the day and claims it can't move."

Tumbo's eyes dart from side to side, and it is obvious he is hiding something.

I turn to find Apondi behind me.

"You and your friends will get everyone in trouble if you go involving yourself in what doesn't concern you," she warns. "Wait until I tell your mother how you are all busy sticking your noses in other people's business. I'll even fetch the switch that she will use to beat your backside raw."

I'm about to tell her to go to hell when a police truck roars in and the crowd draws back. When I turn around, Apondi is gone.

By the time the two policemen load Zgwembe's body into the back of their truck, his father, Rasta, still has not arrived.

"Did anyone go for the poor boy's father?" Apima asks.

"I looked for him in his kiosk, but the man is nowhere to be seen," Amimo says as the police truck roars off.

I try to imagine Rasta learning of his son's death long after it has happened. Though I know he didn't take good care of Zgwembe, I'm sure he loved him like any father would love his son.

CHAPTER TWENTY-SIX

✱ ✱ ✱

TWO MEN STAND ON each side of Zgwembe's grave. They carry shovels with long handles. The skinny one to the left has eyes set close together under a protruding forehead. The other is short, with a thick tuft of hair set on his small head. He pulls out a soiled handkerchief and mops the sweat from his brow.

Zgwembe's father, Rasta, stands next to the coffin, a well-finished brown box with rounded edges and gold handles.

Apima gives a moving eulogy. She speaks of a young life, needlessly cut short.

Our Member of Parliament, Kilo Moja, speaks next. He pumps his hand in the air like he is addressing a political rally. He promises to ensure that those who ended Zgwembe's innocent life will be punished. He lets everyone know that it was him who paid for the coffin and the other expenses. He asks everyone to again vote for him in the coming elections.

"What reason do we have to be proud of these shells we call our bodies?" the priest in a white robe asks. "From dust we are created, to dust we return," he continues, and we bow our heads and nod in agreement.

"In the name of the Father, the Son, and the Holy Spirit," he says, and we all echo, "Amen."

A short woman in a black dress and a matching headscarf stands next to Zgwembe's father. She covers her face and sobs. A girl in a red dress and huge earrings draws the woman close and consoles her. The two embrace, blow their noses, wipe their tears. The girl has a black-and-white framed photo. Its grainy image bears some resemblance to Zgwembe.

"That's the dead boy's mother and sister," someone says. "And of course you know the father, that crook who has a kiosk."

The hired gravediggers shovel dirt into the grave. Their taut muscles ripple under their soiled shirts. Beads of sweat glisten on their foreheads.

"They better pay the guards a little something to guard the grave," Odush says.

"Whatever for?"

"Eh! You didn't know they steal coffins and resell them for fresh burials? Give them a chance and they will dig up the grave, roll Zgwembe out, and steal those new black leather shoes and crisp white shirt they buried him in. If they could sell the body, they would steal that too. Why do they have to dress him up so well when he's dead, anyways? When they couldn't even get him a decent pair of shoes when he was alive? If I were Zgwembe, I'd kick off the shoes, peel off the fancy shirt, and tell them to go to hell," Odush says.

"Who is crazy enough to steal from a corpse? And since when do dead people start getting annoyed and kicking off their shoes?"

"That coffin will still be new for weeks. It can still be sold. And who said dead people don't get annoyed?" Odush says. "There was this man from our village who died here in the city, and they had him all dressed up in a black suit, tie, and fancy things before tucking him into a neat coffin ready to be transported up-country for burial, but the vehicle wouldn't move. Every time the driver fired its engine, revved, and tried to drive off, the engine sputtered then died. Two mechanics gave it a thorough check. They said there was nothing wrong, so everyone was puzzled. Until someone suggested the coffin bearing the dead man should be removed from the vehicle. Immediately the car roared off without a hitch."

Odush pauses long enough for us to puzzle over the first part of his story. He knows we are dying to hear the end of it.

"So the dead man's family conducted prayers, pleaded with him to allow them to transport his body home for burial. That very night he appeared to his widow in a dream and said he was not going home without his Oris watch. He told his widow his cousin had stolen it and that there was no way he was going to allow himself to be transported home until it was returned. Believe it or not, once the watch was recovered and strapped on to the dead man's left wrist, the journey up-country went on without any trouble."

"Now I know you are crazy," I say and Odush smiles.

We file past graves littered with dried carnations.

Zgwembe's mum and sister are still standing by his grave. They haven't moved. They just stand there like they expect him to burrow out of the mound of red earth and announce he hasn't left them. I wonder where they were when he was still alive and needed them.

"Where do people go when they die?" Dado asks in a low tone, almost as though he is thinking aloud. He hasn't said much today.

"Heaven or hell, depending on how good you are," Mose says.

"What if they are still too small to know what's good or bad, like tiny babies?"

"Tiny babies are like angels. They just float into heaven without a hitch," I say.

"My mum tells me I had a twin brother. He never made it out of the hospital after we were born," Dado whispers.

I think of my own baby brother, Banda, his tiny hands curled into fists, eyes half shut, his pink face creased. From the moment Mama returned from the hospital with him swathed in a pink shawl, he never stopped crying. He would scream the whole night and Mama would say it was something called "colic." One morning we awoke to find Mama in tears and baby Banda silent forever.

Mama said he had joined the angels above.

"I think it will rain today," Mose says and breaks the spell.

We file across the road to catch a bus. On the ride back to the estate, no one speaks.

CHAPTER TWENTY-SEVEN

✳ ✳ ✳

"IF MOSE IS COMING ALONG, I'm not going," I tell Dado.

Dado has suggested we make another trip to the abandoned house on Desai Street. There is no way I'm doing it with Mose around after he snitched to his sister and got me in trouble.

"We would have to exclude Odush too. If we ask him along, he'll tell Mose," Dado says.

"Fine," I say, though it no longer sounds like a good idea, just the two of us going to that crazy place. Not that Odush or even Mose can be relied on when there is trouble, but at least four of us sounds safer. But how am I supposed to turn around and say I now want them along when it was me who suggested we go without Mose?

"But what do you expect to find in that haunted house?" I say. "Remember the noise and flashing lights the last time we were there? It might not be such a good idea to visit it at night again."

"That's the only time we can get in there without being seen."

"Seen by who? I thought those ghosts would just sense our presence even if we went at night."

"We need to find out if there really are ghosts in that house. Sometimes I wonder whether ghosts truly exist," Dado says.

I'm about to tell him about the hoofed jinns Uncle Owuoth encountered at the coast, but I decide it isn't such a good idea. Dado would dismiss it as my uncle's drunken talk.

We settle for Sunday when Dado's mother will still be at work and Mama will be at her Women's Guild meeting, which often runs late. Dado will pass by our house at night and whistle twice, so that I know it's him. It all seems scary and exciting at the same time.

THAT MUST BE one of your friends whistling out there," Deno says when the night finally arrives.

I push my comic book under my pillow and slip out through the back door.

"What's wrong with you? My mouth is sore from whistling," Dado complains.

"I was reading a comic and didn't hear."

Outside, the sky is thick and velvety with dark clouds.

Just as we begin to descend from the overpass lightning flashes and the whole of Desai Street is suddenly engulfed in darkness.

Dado and I hesitate.

"Maybe we should do this when there is no blackout," I try for an excuse to put off our visit.

"I'm sure the lights will come . . ." Dado starts to say and suddenly stops in his tracks. "Wait! I think I saw someone up ahead." He grabs my arm as another flash of lightning reveals a dark, hunched figure approaching.

When the sky lights up again we notice that whoever is approaching keeps bending down to collect something from the ground.

"Aaaah! It's only Makaratasi picking up papers," Dado's tone is full of relief.

"I didn't know she operated at night."

"When you are mad you can't tell night from day," Dado says as we hide behind a jacaranda tree to watch Makaratasi go by.

"Did she see us?"

"Does it matter? Even if she did, she'd probably not remember," Dado says just as the streetlamps come back on, bathing the whole street in light.

I reach into my pocket and run my fingers against a penknife I pinched from Deno's backpack. I'm not certain why I took it, but knowing it's in my pocket is reassuring.

The distant roar of a car spurs us into hiding behind a bougainvillea bush a couple meters from the gate to the deserted house. The car's headlights bounce against the green gate as it grinds to a halt. A man jumps out from the passenger seat to open the gate, which lets out a loud screech.

The car drives in, but the gate remains open.

"Come on!" Dado grabs my arm and we dash into the compound through the open gate. "Let's go to the back and see what's happening."

"I don't think it's a good idea," I protest, but Dado is already moving and tugging me along.

Every shadow seems sinister, every sound a threat.

Dado squats under a window ledge and tells me to climb onto his shoulders.

"What do you see in there?"

I press my face against the cold windowpane, but I can't see a thing in the darkness.

"Get down, someone's coming," Dado whispers, and I leap down to the ground. We hide behind a huge metal water tank, just as the back door to the house opens.

A tall man steps out. A shorter fellow in an oversize jacket joins him.

"But that's Mwachuma!" I whisper, and Dado elbows me into silence.

The short man strikes a match and raises it to light a cigarette. From the glow on his face it is obviously Mwachuma—there is no mistaking him with the black eye patch. He sucks at his cigarette and bursts into a fit of coughing.

"You should go easy on those cigarettes," the tall man says.

Mwachuma finishes his cigarette, crushes it underfoot.

A third man joins them, and I almost don't believe my eyes.

"Tumbo," I whisper, and it is more of a statement than a question, because this third short, squat man is none other than our estate overseer.

"We need to find another place to operate from," Mwachuma says. "There is too much attention on us."

"If you had driven that lorry yourself, instead of allowing that lunatic Rasta to drive it, we would not have attracted so much attention," the tall man reasons.

"It's not only because of the accident that the police are mad," Mwachuma says. "Are you forgetting that one of your men was shot and injured, while the other was arrested by the police? That's what heated things up."

"That idiot deserved it. How do you try to pull such a stunt in broad daylight?" The tall guy raises his voice.

"Now that the police have that lorry and know it's mine, I can't go back to my yard. So how am I supposed to operate? Trust me, things can only get worse."

"Our man at the police station told me some kid handed them a photo and diary that belonged to Swiney. The kid claimed they found it in an old car that once belonged to the dead man," the tall man says, and it's obvious that Dado is as surprised as I am because he nudges me hard.

"Must be those nosy kids in the estate. What exactly was in the diary?" Mwachuma lights another cigarette, sucks at it, and bursts into a fresh spell of coughing. He tosses it into the dark, the glowing butt floating into the night and almost landing on my head.

"The man wrote that he was threatened. He doesn't name names but he mentions someone with a black eye patch," the tall man chuckles. "But it's the death of that man called Stingo that has the police hopping mad. The man was an undercover officer," the tall man lowers his voice.

"That guy was asking too many questions. Something had to be done about him," Tumbo says.

"Anyway, I spoke to the boss and he says he is arranging for an alternative transit point. Now we better get back to work," the tall man turns and walks back into the house.

The others follow after a spell.

We stay behind the water tank, too stunned to move. I'm shocked, as I'm certain Dado is, that the diary and photo have been handed in to the police. My mind is racing through all the stuff I've heard, trying to process it. It's only after Dado elbows me that I snap back to the present.

Dado crawls through the hole in the hedge and I'm right behind him.

We hurry down Desai Street and across the overpass without a word. We don't stop until we reach the estate and even then we are still silent.

"Do you think we should tell Odush or Mose what we heard?" I finally ask Dado.

"Let's sleep on it and talk about it tomorrow," Dado says, as if it will even be possible to find sleep after what we heard.

"Alright," I agree. "Goodnight."

"Goodnight," Dado says and melts away into the dark.

I tap on our bedroom window and Deno lets me in through the back door.

CHAPTER TWENTY-EIGHT

✳ ✳ ✳

BUMBLES WARNS ME that tomorrow's holiday has yet to begin and
that I should stop daydreaming in class.

I'm not alone. Everyone is excited over the upcoming national
holiday. But that's not the reason I can't concentrate. The reason is,
I'm still stunned by last night's events at the house on Desai Street.
It's the reason I'm distracted from what Bumbles is teaching. I
wonder if Dado is doing any better down at St. Josephs.

The final bell goes and we are off from our seats like they have
tacks on them.

Bumbles slaps a textbook hard against his desk to catch our
attention, and we sink back down.

"This here is a classroom and not a beer hall. Now I want you
to rise and leave in an orderly manner," he barks.

We observe some restraint until we hit the door and then we
are scrambling down the hallway and out past the main gate like
we are scared we might be summoned back to class.

At the estate I slip out of my uniform and rush out before
Mama cooks up some chore that needs doing. Outside, the sun is

a dull orange ball in the distance. And, yes, my friends are already behind the estate, sitting on the Zephyr.

Dado rises from the hood of the car and paces up and down. "I don't want anything to do with you anymore," he waves a hand at Odush.

"But I'm the one who found the photo and diary. I had the right to do with them as I pleased," Odush scowls.

"Is this guy serious?" Dado shakes his head.

Odush has admitted to handing over the photo and diary to the police. He thinks he did the right thing.

"And you. Will you ever learn to keep a secret?" Odush turns to Mose.

"But it's not me who told them," Mose protests.

"Mose didn't tell us anything," Dado says.

"He is the only one who knew I surrendered the diary," Odush says.

"Not exactly," Dado whispers under his breath and glances at me. "Now that you gave the police the photo and the diary, what have they done? Thanks to you, Mwachuma and his crooks will know that we are on to them."

"And who said the police will tell them? The police are probably investigating and will arrest them soon," Odush says.

"Let's wait and see," Dado starts to walk away. "And you better cross your fingers Mwachuma doesn't come for you at night to slit your throat with his Okapi knife," he slides his forefinger across his throat.

THE NEXT DAY IS the 1st of June, Madaraka Day. It's the day the British allowed our country to rule itself.

The celebration is reflected in the flags and banners that cover every conceivable place in the estate. They flutter from below the rafters of the overseer's office and the entrance of the social hall. The burglar-proofed windows of the estate pub are also covered in four-colored banners. Even Mama Nandwa's kiosk has a tattered old flag at the entrance.

Ours is a four-colored flag—black is for the people, green for the land, red for the blood we shed, and then there is white.

White is for peace. Defeated people pull out white flags when they surrender and they don't want to fight anymore. At least that's what Deno says.

But we weren't defeated. We won our independence from the British. So then what's the white on our flag for?

It is possible that after fighting for so long our leaders decided: *never again*. Could be that's what the white is for.

I hate our flag, which is not the same as hating our country. It's just that each time the flag is raised you have to stand ramrod straight or you are in trouble. It doesn't matter if there is a bee in your face or snot running down your nose. Even if there are safari ants crawling up your pants, you move, you're in trouble.

Sometimes you're just on your way to some place without any pesky flags on your mind, when someone blows a whistle because they are hoisting a dirty, tattered flag, and you have no choice but to stand to attention until the thing is up.

We raise flags in school. During morning parade a scout marches forward to flash a salute that doesn't even look like the real salutes soldiers execute on national days. He unfurls a flag and we stand to attention until it is up and fluttering.

Our Headie says honoring our flag makes us patriotic. Most people want the country to do everything for them but they haven't done anything for it.

"'Ask not what your country can do for you,'" our Headie looks out above our heads and mimics someone else's voice. He asks, "Do you know who said those words?"

Of course we know because he has asked us many times before. They are the words of an American president who was shot by one of his citizens, because they all have guns and are allowed to use them for self-defense. How can shooting a president, who is just waving at people, be self-defense? But that is America, and in America people have rights, even if it is the right to shoot you dead.

Our Headie says, "This was Kennedy, a president much loved by his people."

Then why would they shoot him, if they loved him so much?

But again, that is America, and in America people do things that don't make sense unless you're American.

Raising the flag is about respect for your country. That is what we are taught in school. But who says you can force people to respect something? They will only pretend, and when no one is watching they'll use the flag to wipe their dirty backsides and then there will be a fifth color on it.

I've seen films where people strut around in pants made with the Union Jack—which is what Bumbles calls the British flag. In my country, they would probably shoot me if I did that.

BABA WORKS ON national holidays since his is an essential service. "Trains must run even when everyone else is celebrating. If all the trains stopped moving for even a day, there would be a shortage of essential commodities and the country would grind to a halt," Baba pushes his chest out to show how important his work is.

I switch on Baba's radio and twist its dials until it hits the right spot.

"*Woi!*

Woi!

Woi tunataka Kenyatta aachiliwe"—the radio blares out song after song about the Father of the Nation. The songs go on about how he was humiliated and jailed but did not give up his fight for our independence.

In school we are taught that there were others who also fought for independence. Nobody is singing about them, though. Maybe they didn't fight as hard as the Father of the Nation.

A man with a loud, commanding voice on the radio announces what is going on at the celebrations. He calls out the names of the different groups in his bossy tone. He calls someone to narrate a shairi for the Father of the Nation, and you can tell from the poet's voice that she is a girl. She praises the Father of the Nation until the man with the commanding voice stops her so someone else can also praise the Father of the Nation. The next person drones on like a group of bumblebees.

Fighter jets roar past and I can feel the whole house shake. I rush outside to find Mose and Dado standing next to Block 10. Odush stands a couple of meters away from them. Yesterday's tension over the photo and diary is far from over.

We crane our necks and watch the silver jets do flips. The first does a double flip then tears up into the clouds. The second rolls over like a playful puppy that wants its belly tickled, then straightens and shoots up into the clouds. The third flips once, twice, even a third time, but does not rise out of it, and at first I'm thinking, *he's the best*, until a dull distant thud followed by a ball of fire announces that the plane has crashed. A thick pall of smoke rises from where it went down.

"Bloody old secondhand jets those whites sold us," someone says.

"No, it's our pilots who can't do anything right. They should have let the whites continue to fly those damn things."

"Don't go blaming the pilots or the people that sold the planes. It's the crooks that run this country. Trust them to go and buy scrap metal instead of planes, just so they can line their pockets," a woman with a colorful lesso around her wide bosom says.

"The pilot probably bailed out before the plane hit the ground," Dado says. "They have seats that eject from the plane with the pilot strapped to it."

"Eish! And who do you expect to believe that?" the woman in a lesso asks and walks away.

Dado is talking about the pilots who shoot out of burning planes in war films. But that's acting. This here is real, with the smoke still thick and rising. Worst of all, we see no parachute in the sky.

"If he jumped out we'd have seen him float down in a parachute," I say.

"Just because the plane looked like it was close by doesn't mean it was. Those things move so fast, one minute it's here in Nairobi, the next it is in Mombasa. Perhaps he jumped out miles away from here, and right now he is on the ground gathering up his parachute, laughing at everyone who thinks he is dead."

"But the smoke looks like it was from across the bridge, and not too far off."

We continue to argue about the pilot, whether he is alive, about the distance, the cause of the crash. Everyone has their own story of what brought the jet down. Someone even says it was shot down and that they saw something streak out from the ground before the jet burst into flames. I want to scream, *it's a bloody lie*, but people usually believe what they want to, so I just let it go.

When I return to our living room the Father of the Nation is speaking on the radio. He reminds everyone of the sacrifices that led to independence. He fishes out his most threatening voice when warning those he calls wasaliti. Those are the traitors who work with foreigners to bring the country down. He shouts "Haraaaambeee," and the crowd's response makes Baba's radio cackle. He threatens to pound the enemies of the state to dust. He talks of himself in the third person, like he is speaking about someone else. After a long speech, he again shouts "Haraaambee," but this time the response is not as loud as before. I guess people are tired and hungry, and need to leave. I've heard it said that you can't leave the venue before the Father of the Nation does.

BABA NO LONGER TAKES us to watch the march during national celebrations. He says he is too busy, but I've heard him tell Mama that it has become too politicized and dangerous, whatever that means.

I loved watching the march, how the soldiers tilted their faces to look at the cheering crowd. These days I just listen to it on the radio.

Mama celebrates by powdering her face and straightening her hair with a hot comb. She wears her favorite kitenge, and makes Apondi cook chapatis, rice, and chicken, which we wash down with TreeTop juice.

All national days are about how we outfoxed the white settlers. The Father of the Nation says that independence was not given to us on a platter. Lots of blood was shed, and therefore we must be ready to defend it. He swings his flywhisk above his head and threatens anyone who would even think of disrupting our hard-earned uhuru. The Father of the Nation has people everywhere who see and hear everything. Baba says all the people who work for the government are his eyes and ears.

His picture is on coins and banknotes, on office walls, in classrooms, hospitals, hotels, airports, people's living rooms, everywhere. We always pray to God to give the Father of the Nation the strength to rule our land and nation. I stare up at his portrait on our wall and marvel at his fierce eyes and big beard that looks like a lion's mane. I listen to his booming voice on Baba's radio, and I am convinced our country is safe.

"MY FATHER SAYS you can't look into the eyes of the Father of the Nation." Mose wears a solemn look as he speaks.

"And what happens if you do?"

"I don't know, but my father says it is never done. Maybe you'd go blind," Mose laughs.

"So how are you supposed to work with him if you can't look him in the eye?"

"Who told you the Father of the Nation works? He only gives orders and makes declarations," Mose says.

"Of course that's work. Even managers give orders. Doesn't mean they don't work," I say.

"Now just because your father is a manager you are comparing managers with the Father of the Nation?" Mose eyes me like I've committed a sin, and I back off.

I don't want them thinking I'm showing off.

CHAPTER TWENTY-NINE

*** * ***

A POLICEMAN IN FULL UNIFORM, complete with a hat and whistle, comes to our house one evening. He must have been waiting outside, because I barely slip off my knapsack and school tie when he knocks on the front door. He has a notebook and a blue pen.

He asks what I know about Mwachuma and the Bedford lorry that was pulled out of the ditch. I can tell from his questions that he has already spoken to Mose or Odush who have told him all they know. It's obvious he doesn't know about Mwachuma's connection to the deserted house.

Mama hovers around and doesn't leave me alone with him.

"Have you ever seen Mwachuma driving that green Bedford lorry?" the policeman asks for the second time.

"He's already told you that he has never seen anyone driving the lorry," Mama interjects. "Unless you are asking him to lie, and I didn't bring my kids up that way," she clucks.

"But your friend, what's his name . . ." the policeman consults his notebook. "Yes . . . Odush said the lorry was in that man's yard and that there were fresh tire marks?"

"Everyone knows that lorry was parked in that crook's yard," Mama interjects.

After the policeman realizes he's not going to get anything new from me he folds his notebook to leave. Mama offers him tea but I can tell from her tone she doesn't mean it. I think the policeman also knows, because he shakes his head and walks out.

"Now you see why I keep telling you to stay indoors and read your books instead of poking your nose in other people's business?" Mama says after the man has gone. "Next time the police come calling I'll not concern myself with big-headed fools who do not listen to their parents. Your father and I have never had policemen walking in and out of our house. What do you think the neighbors will say?"

The way she talks, you would think a whole squad of policemen has been investigating our house.

"GO ON, tell your father about the police coming to our house today," Mama corners me into recounting the visit to Baba.

"Young man, you better stay off this Mwachuma business," Baba says, reaching for the dial of his radio.

Mama's face twists into a frown, and you can tell she doesn't think Baba is taking the whole thing seriously enough. She turns to give me one of her *this is far from over* looks and storms off to the kitchen.

IT'S A SATURDAY, and there is no school for me or detention because the new demerits on my conduct card have not reached three.

The ring of the newspaper vendor's bicycle bell pierces the morning and I dash out to get Baba's paper.

There is a picture of Idi Amin frowning on the front page. His army uniform is weighed down by medals.

"Lumumba, can I have my paper?" Baba shouts from the living room and I rush in to hand it to him.

"Amin has ordered his soldiers to shoot anyone found smuggling coffee across the border. People are now trooping to some place called 'Chepkube' near the Uganda border to smuggle the 'black gold,' as coffee is now called," Baba reads from his paper.

"Why has everyone gone crazy about coffee?" Mama wants to know. "All these years people have grown it and no one has even noticed. Now they are willing to kill for it."

"It's because Brazil, the biggest producer of coffee, lost most of its crop due to bad weather. Someone has to feed the white man's hunger for coffee," Baba lifts his head from his paper.

Wow! So these Brazilians do things other than playing football. I know about Pele and how he is the best football player in the world. But I didn't know about their coffee. I can tell from Mama's face that she too didn't know. I can't wait to show off to Dado and Mose about how Brazil's coffee has been destroyed and now places like Uganda are cashing in.

CHAPTER THIRTY

✳ ✳ ✳

I DO NOT SEE NJISH UNTIL she almost knocks me over. She looks smart in her green pleated dress with a huge white buckle at the waist. She takes my hand in hers and I look around to see if anyone is watching. Her face is radiant, her dimples round and sweet. We steal glances at each other but mostly look down into the ground when our eyes meet.

"We'll be leaving for America soon. My father says there are more opportunities there," she says.

"America, America?"

"Yes, America," Njish nods.

We remain silent, but my heart is beating so loud I'm scared she will hear the thumping sound. She squeezes my hand, and though I want to squeeze back, my muscles won't move. My whole body is frozen still.

"America is a good place," I say, as if I have ever been there. I'm not even certain why I say it. I've heard that people who go to America get lost and never come back.

"We'll write each other?" She brushes her other hand against mine and my mind is racing. "I'll send you pictures from America."

"Good," I say and we stay silent.

When I steal another look at her, I see tears in her big round eyes.

"I have something for you," she whispers and slips a small beaded bracelet onto my wrist.

I am still admiring it when, from nowhere, Apondi appears and Njish snatches her hand back and hurries away.

"Ah! There you are," Apondi says.

"What is it you want?"

"You think I don't know what you and that girl are up to? Your father pays so much money to have you in that nice school and still you have to hang around with that useless girl. She is not even one of us. They are not our people."

"Njish is not useless," I protest but Apondi is already walking away.

I'm still rooted to the spot, my mind blank and my lips quivering, when I feel a faint touch to my shoulder. I jump and I'm about to cry out, only to find it's Njish. I can tell from the look on her face that she heard what Apondi said.

"Why does she hate me?"

"Forget Apondi! She says things she doesn't mean," I reply quickly.

"My mother also says you are not one of us. She says you're different, and that your people are always making trouble. But I don't care. I still like you more than anyone."

I try to think of something to say, but I can't find the words. I always thought the reason Njish's mother looked at me funny was because we are always darting about the estate causing trouble. I didn't know it was me she didn't like.

"Don't think much of those grown-ups. They are always complaining about one thing or the other," I finally say.

"Are you different?"

"Of course I'm different. I'm a boy and you're a girl."

"I mean different from, say, Mose. My mum likes him. She says they are our people."

"Grown-ups make a big deal about little things like where people come from, but who cares."

"I also don't care," she says and starts to walk away. She turns and there is this beautiful smile on her face.

"You will wait for me until I come back from America?"

I nod.

"And stay away from that Hill School girl, Lillian," she says, and is gone.

I stand rooted to the spot.

I'VE BEEN COMPOSING a letter for Njish. I've been at it for a long time. Some of the words I intend to use are from Baba's Oxford dictionary. I wait until there is no one in the living room and then I pull it out from the top of Baba's bookshelf. I flip through it in my room looking for words to impress Njish.

I have a few words I've settled on like "affection" and "passion." However, I have doubts about "passion" because it sounds a bit too grown-up-ish. I don't want Njish thinking I am like those dirty men who spend their time next to the social hall hurling out dirty words after they are tipsy from drinking beer.

I've not written down any of the words. I have them stored in my head where nosy people like Awino and Apondi cannot find them. Now that Njish is going to America I guess I'll just leave them there till she comes back, even though I'm not sure when that will be. But I'll wait because I like her and she likes me.

I once saw a man go down on his knee and ask a woman to marry him. Though it was only in a film it looked good. When Njish comes back and we are old enough, I will wait until we are alone and go down on my knee to ask her to marry me. Then we will live in a big house and have children.

CHAPTER THIRTY-ONE

✳ ✳ ✳

WE PLAN TO VISIT the house on Desai Street again tomorrow night. Even though we know it isn't haunted, the idea of visiting it is no less scary. If Tumbo and the other crooks could get rid of Stingo for asking too many questions, imagine what they could do to us.

"The more people we are, the greater the likelihood of being caught. And besides why did he have to hand over the photo and diary to the police behind our backs?" Dado argues why he does not want Odush along. He has followed me all the way to Amimo's shed where I have gone to buy charcoal for Mama.

But we also went to the house on Desai Street without telling them, I want to say, but I don't. After all, it was my idea to exclude Mose the last time.

"We need Odush in case we are cornered. You know the way he sprints off like an impala, he could run away and get help," I say. "Besides we've always done things together. We're a team and it should stay that way," I continue.

"Then we will have to tell them about our last visit and what we discovered," Dado concedes. "Wait until they learn that the only ghosts in that house are Mwachuma, Tumbo, and their gang of crooks," he laughs.

"YOU'RE LYING," Mose says and waves his hand.

We have just told them about our last visit to the house on Desai Street and what we heard Mwachuma, Tumbo, and the tall guy say.

"You want to say that all along it was those crooks who have been pretending to be ghosts, and that you heard them talking about the diary we found, and that Stingo was a police officer and all that other stuff? Man, that's crazy." Mose pauses to catch his breath.

"Yes, that's the reason we need to get to the bottom of it all, so that the thieves can be arrested before they come for Odush who handed over our diary."

"I don't believe you. You've made it all up to scare us. How do we know that you actually visited the ghost house?" Odush says, but he is unable to hide the concern on his face.

"We're going back tonight. If you aren't too scared to come along, you can join us. Otherwise you can stay at home shivering and waiting for Mwachuma and Tumbo to come and slit your throat. Or maybe they'll just knock you out and light a charcoal jiko next to you like they did with Stingo. I've heard that death from carbon monoxide poisoning is painless. You just fall asleep and you never wake up," Dado sneers.

"And who said I'm afraid of Mwachuma? I'm definitely coming along," Odush says, slapping his chest hard.

"Me too," Mose shouts.

"And afterward you can snitch on us to your little sister," I sneer at Mose.

"That only happened once and I said I'm sorry," Mose averts his eyes.

"Now here is a sketch of the compound of that house." Dado gets down on his haunches. He uses a broken twig to draw on the dusty ground. "This here is the hole in the hedge," he makes an "X" with his twig. "This is the house with a door in the front and at the back." He marks a "D" at the two spots. "And this here is the big water tank behind which we hid the last time." He marks a "W." "I suggest one of us stays on the street outside the compound, ready to run and get help if we're caught." Dado looks in Odush's direction. "You can hide behind the bougainvillea bush." He marks a "B" on his sketch.

"Why should I be the one to stay outside?" Odush complains, but there is little conviction in his tone.

"Any one of us can be out there. We could decide for Mose to be there, or even me," Dado says.

"I'll stay outside," Mose offers.

"No, we already decided I'll be the one to stay outside. After all, I can run faster than you," Odush says quickly, and we all laugh.

"So that's settled," Dado continues. "Now, if we're caught and we scream for help, run to the police station and tell them everything, including what Lumush and I heard the last time. Tell them we heard the men talk about how Stingo had to be silenced. That will certainly have them acting," he says.

"We meet behind the slaughterhouse at nine o'clock p.m."

"Yes, see you then," I say. That will be a good time for me. It's when Baba listens to the news after we've had supper. It won't be difficult to excuse myself like I'm off to bed and slip out unnoticed.

MOSE SHOWS UP last behind the slaughterhouse. We had decided against meeting near the Zephyr because everyone knows it's our spot and we don't want Apondi or someone else interrupting.

Above, a playful silver moon peeps out from inside a thick blanket of clouds. A distant blare of a locomotive adds to the gloom. There is barely any activity on Desai Street.

When we get to the spot near the bougainvillea bush, Dado signals us to stop.

"From here you will be able to see anyone entering the compound," Dado says, slapping Odush on the shoulder. "Make sure you keep as close to the hedge as possible so no one sees you. One whistle blast will be a warning that someone's coming in. You hear us shout for help, sprint to the police station. Tell them what we heard the men say, especially about Stingo. That should make them do something. And Mose, you stay behind Lumush. Not now please, just stick to the plan," he cuts Mose short when he tries to speak.

"Why don't you let him say what he wants to say?" Odush says, but Dado is already on the move.

He goes down on his knees and crawls through the gap in the hedge. I follow closely, stopping only to dislodge a barb caught in my jacket, then I'm through.

"Let's head for the back," Dado tugs at my arm. We keep off the graveled drive to avoid the *crunch, crunch* sound against our feet.

"Shhhh. Did you hear that?"

"It's only a cat," Dado says, as a white cat slips past.

I remember Uncle Owuoth once telling me about jinns transforming themselves into cats to lure unsuspecting victims. However, now we know we aren't dealing with ghosts so I don't give the cat much thought. By the time we get to the back of the compound, the moon above has found some empty space between the clouds, increasing our visibility.

Dado crouches and runs forward. He reaches for the door, opens it, and pulls out a flashlight I didn't know he had and switches it on. Its beam bounces into the room, revealing sacks piled on top of each other.

"Someone in there is bound to see that light . . ." I start to whisper before the night's quiet is shattered by loud barking from behind us and all I can think of is Mwachuma's mongrel, Tarzan, ripping us apart.

"Run!" I shout, and Dado bumps into me, knocking me to the ground.

I rise, slip, and fall down again. The barking and growling are now right in my face, as a warm, yeasty smell fills my nostrils. I think I'm finished, but the barking recedes as suddenly as it began.

I'm up again, and my heart feels like it wants to jump right out of my chest. A couple of steps and I bump into something, someone who grunts and grabs me by my shoulder, flinging me to the ground. I struggle to my feet before a heavy blow explodes on the side of my head, and my legs no longer feel the ground below. A second blow lights up a thousand stars in my head, and then I'm drifting, sinking into nothing.

MY HEAD THROBS. My throat is dry. My hands are bound behind my back. My feet are tied together. I try to move my mouth but I can't. Something tight bites against its sides. I try to blink away the pain.

I hear the sound of feet scuffing against the floor, followed by whispers:

"We need to move the coffee out of this place before light. I've already arranged for a lorry which will be here soon," one of the men says, his voice loud and commanding.

"I hope you've also arranged for loaders. There are too many sacks and they're too heavy. It would take too long to load them into a lorry. We don't have time," another one says, and though his tone is guarded, it is obviously Tumbo. "And what do we do with the two kids?" he asks.

I'm relieved. At least I'm not alone, I think, before a sense of guilt hits me.

"You leave that to me. For now let's make this coffee disappear," the loud one says with finality.

A door slams shut.

"Lumush! Lumush!"

I hear Dado's voice and I feel a burst of energy. I try to speak but I can't because something tight rips across my mouth.

"Are you gagged?"

"Mmm . . ." I mumble.

"I was gagged too, but I slipped it off. Keep moving your mouth up and down and the gag will drop," Dado lowers his voice.

I move my mouth up, down, and sideways to try and loosen my gag, but it just won't move. I keep on doing that until my mouth is sore.

"Roll over so I can use my teeth to untie you," Dado whispers, and I roll over toward him.

After a lot of maneuvering I feel his warm breath on my wrists as he gnaws at the knots that bind them. Soon his breath is labored, but still he works at it. After what seems like forever, the knots loosen and my arms are free. I rip off the gag and get to work. It does not take me long to untie the knots on Dado's arms.

"We better get out of here." I grope for the door, but it's locked.

"Easy now, they'll hear you," Dado whispers, and at that very moment the lights come on.

"And where do you two think you are going?" Tumbo stands at the door with a metal bar in his hand.

He is joined by the tall man we saw the last time. And Mwachuma.

"Now you'll learn why you should never interfere in other people's business," Tumbo raises the metal bar and advances.

"Our friends have gone for the police." Dado steps back. His tone is steady and that surprises me, because I'm shaking and my heart is racing.

Tumbo stops in his tracks.

"Oh yes!" Dado nods. "At this very moment, Odush and Mose are telling the police where to find Stingo's killers."

"Who told you about Stingo?" Tumbo lowers his arm.

"Ah! You mean, how did we know about the charcoal jiko and the carbon monoxide poisoning?" Dado's voice rises.

The tall man hasn't said a word but gestures Tumbo aside, and it is at that moment that the sound of sirens fills the night.

"Now you see what I meant?" Dado shouts out, but the three men are already fighting to get out through the back door.

"Down! All of you, down!" someone shouts from outside.

Tumbo rushes back in, followed by a uniformed policeman with a gun in his hand.

"Don't you move." The policeman points the gun at Tumbo, who drops the metal bar and raises his hands in surrender.

"The boys are in here," the policeman shouts out and is joined by another. "Don't worry, we're police officers," one of them says. As if it isn't obvious.

"YOU TWO HAVE your friends to thank," a burly police officer says after we're freed, opening the back door of a police car. A blue light flashing from its roof gives the compound a surreal look.

The officer directs the beam of his flashlight at three hand-cuffed men seated on the grass. Tumbo and the tall man avert their faces, but Mwachuma stares up at them defiantly.

"I've never been inside a police car," I whisper to Dado, and I'm sure it's also his first time.

Raindrops begin to dot the windshield.

"Time to get you boys home," one of the officers fires the car's engine. "Someone will visit you tomorrow to record your statements," he says as he steers the car out of the compound.

"Wait until Mose and Odush hear that we got a lift in a police car," Dado nudges me and smiles.

CHAPTER THIRTY-TWO

✳ ✳ ✳

IT IS NOW ONE WEEK since we were rescued from the house on Desai Street. Dado, Odush, and Mose are seated with me in our living room. It's strange that despite being friends for so many years, it's the first time we are all together in our house.

Mama convinced Baba to take time off from work because today is an important day.

There is a knock at the door, and I answer it even before Mama asks.

I open the main door to find Bumbles standing there and I'm stunned. What could Bumbles of all people be doing in Railway Estate on a Saturday, and worse still at our doorstep?

"Good morning, Lumumba," Bumbles extends his hand and shakes mine like we are the best of friends.

Not waiting for an invitation, he walks right into our living room, and it is clear from the way Mama and Baba welcome him that they have been expecting him.

"Now, won't you introduce me to your friends," he says, but

Mama is already at it, reeling out names before retreating to the kitchen.

After she is gone, Baba and Bumbles go on and on about African history, which they both seem fond of. It's almost noon when a neat blue Mercedes pulls up outside our house. A police officer leaps out, opening the back door to let out a tall man in a smart blue uniform. You can tell from the way the officers mill around him, saluting, that he is their boss.

They usher him into our living room where Mama, Baba, and Bumbles rise to greet him.

Baba leads him to the green chair next to the radio. He removes his hat, balances it on his knee, and introduces himself as an assistant commissioner of police.

"These must be the brave boys I've heard so much about," he says, looking in our direction.

"Oh yes!" Bumbles nods. "The one to the left is my student. A very bright boy," he says, and Mama's smile lights up the room.

"You must be Mr. Bumbles," the assistant commissioner turns in his direction. "I'm sorry about your brother, but now, thanks to these young men, the culprits will finally be brought to justice."

The assistant commissioner then informs us that Mwachuma and the other thugs have confessed to running a coffee smuggling ring. "They have also confessed to being responsible for the deaths of Mr. Swiney and his family, as my men earlier informed Mr. Bumbles."

Bumbles takes off his glasses and uses a handkerchief to wipe his eyes.

"My officers have already communicated the details to Mr. Bumbles, so I need not go into that. All I'll add, which I'm sure the brave boys already know, is that we also lost a dedicated officer called Stingo who was working undercover. I'd like to again thank you boys for your bravery. I will be forwarding your names for the Presidential Award. But that doesn't mean you should take such risks in future." The man smiles and sips the tea Mama has served him. "Next time just report whatever you suspect to the police and let us do the investigating."

AFTER THE ASSISTANT commissioner is gone, Mama warns us about poking our noses into other people's business. She tries as hard as possible to wear a stern face, but she can't hide the pride in her eyes.

"There are some mandazis I baked for you boys, but that doesn't mean you can go creeping into deserted houses in the middle of the night. You could get yourselves killed." She smiles, as though what she just said is amusing.

"Lumumba?"

"Yes Ma . . ."

"Why don't you see your teacher out?" Mama says, when Bumbles rises to leave.

"Thank you," Bumbles turns and says.

He hugs me, and though he averts his face, I know there are tears welling down his cheeks.

Then I watch his hunched figure recede in the gathering dusk.

"SO TELL US HOW you were gagged by the thieves," Mose says, edging closer.

"But we already told you a hundred times." I slide off the hood of the Zephyr.

Up ahead, the sun is steadily sinking. I know Apondi will soon be along to tell me Mama wants me indoors, and that the evil car will finally be our undoing.

"I want to hear it again. I want to hear how they bound your hands and feet like kidnappers do in films. Is it also true you were attacked by dogs? Now that's cool," he says.

But no one is listening because Odush and Dado are already arm wrestling on the car's hood, and my bet is on Dado.

THE END

ABOUT THE AUTHOR

Patrick Ochieng is a lawyer and author who was shortlisted for the 2010 Golden Baobab Prize and longlisted for the Syncity NG 2018 Anthology Prize. He has been published in *Kikwetu*, *Munyori*, *Brittle Paper*, and other literary publications. He lives in Kenya with his family.

ABOUT ACCORD BOOKS

Accord works with authors from across the African continent to provide support throughout the writing process and secure regional and international publishing and distribution for their works. We believe that stories are both life-affirming and life-enhancing, and want to see a world where all children are delighted and enriched by incredible stories written by African authors.